Vision Dreams

A PARABLE

ANTHONY R. CANDELA

ISBN 978-1-0980-0673-0 (paperback)
ISBN 978-1-0980-0674-7 (digital)

Christian Faith Publishing, Inc.
832 Park Avenue
Meadville, PA 16335
www.christianfaithpublishing.com

Printed in the United States of America

Dreams are but interludes which fancy makes.
—Dryden

Our truest life is when we are
in our dreams awake.
—Thoreau

PROLOGUE

Somewhere in the Universe

"Flatline! We've got a flatline!"

English is such a wonderful language. A single word can not only describe a phenomenon but also its action and appearance.

Although I am uncertain of my current whereabouts in the universe or whether I am alive or dead, somehow I have assumed a strange kind of omniscience. I don't know how I know, but I can tell you that a few of my friends fared worse than me. Of this, I am certain the only thing more daunting than watching yourself being worked on by frantic emergency room surgeons is watching them fail. It's the last thing I remember—that is, until now.

The man behind the mask shouted, "This is the third time he's flatlined in the past ten minutes."

A woman from behind a second mask glanced anxiously at a monitor. "I've never seen this technology before. We can't handle this."

Helpless and bewildered and observing these events from a vantage point far from the actual proceedings, I began to feel palpably nauseated. Hovering as it seemed above the fracas and at a distance from what was happening, it was uncanny that the woman's tone could affect me so.

A voice spoke. It was mine, but I don't think anyone heard. "How can this be happening? Where am I? Inside my body or am I really up here looking down on this crazy scene?"

The man leaned forward and looked inside my skull through the lenses of a head-mounted viewer. The contraption was attached to a thin transparent fiber of drawn glass that disappeared into the back of my head. His hands rested on a small panel; thumbs and fingers manipulated controls. His expression evinced incredulity as he struggled to terminate the events unfolding before him. As I watched, a sad look of resignation flooded his eyes, percolating it seemed, from the depths of his soul.

"They're all over the occipital lobe and moving at random," he shouted. "I can't get a single target lock." The doctor sounded exasperated. "They've torn apart half the lobe, and I'm doing almost as much harm with this laser as those microscopic bastards are doing with their rampage."

The doctor worked furiously for what seemed like an eternity. Then came the coup de grâce. My cerebral invaders prepared their final blow. Apparently intending to snuff out the last vestiges of my conscious awareness, if not my existence, they rapidly migrated south and made ready to skewer my brain stem.

The doctor's voice faded into the distance. Straightening, his hands dropped to his side. Sweat poured from his brow and intermingled with tears flowing from his eyes. His voice echoed and reverberated first from within my cranium and then from without. I heard him say, "Damn it! It's over."

CHAPTER 1

Dreams

They were any parents. Life brought them together, and they made a baby. They prepared to spend the next nine months and twenty-one years helping him fulfill his dreams—and perhaps, if things went well, a few of their own. However, as is often the case when a child comes into the world, there are surprises, and life trajectories change.

I was born blind. In retrospect, my parents shouldn't have been surprised that something untoward happened, but they were. After all, they had the same option to undertake genetic screening as everyone else, but because they had never heard of a single-birth defect in their families, and because they felt nature should be allowed to take its course, they decided to forego the procedure. Faced with reality, my dad had his hands full. Not only were his own aspirations for me dashed, his wife was quite upset.

"It will be all right." Dad held me in one arm and Mom in the other. "First, we've got to figure out what to do, and then we'll sue these idiots for allowing this to happen."

"They told us our baby was fine," she said. "Now they tell us there's nothing to do but find a special school for him. They've washed their hands of us."

Although not an unheard-of event, at the time of my entrance into the world, it had become rare for someone to be born with less than perfect attributes. Although modern medical science could prevent most prenatal problems, it hadn't caught them all. While genetic prescreening reduced the number of babies born with "defects," the attention society gave to helping those the medical "safety-net" failed to protect was proportionally reduced. Babies born without vision or hearing, missing one or more of their limbs, or even worse, fell victim to dwindling services that might help them and their parents cope with life. Later, because of a protracted an unfortunate war, so did the availability of technology that would have at least facilitated these children getting along in the world they inherited.

"Let's go home," Dad said. "Let's take our son home and make sure we don't make any more mistakes."

Mom sobbed. "He was going to be the ballplayer you would have been, had you gotten the right breaks. You were so happy when they told us we were going to have a son. You lit up every time you talked about teaching him to play."

"That was a pipe dream," Dad retorted. "How many kids are born with just the right talent?"

"I know," Mom answered, "but now we'll never know." Then looking into his eyes as he drove them home, she asked, "How are you feeling now?"

Dad didn't answer. He didn't know. Then he said, "I guess he'll be a handful, but we'll figure out something for him to do."

Turning to his wife, Dad asked, "How about you? How are you feeling?"

She answered, "I'm numb. I feel him in my arms, and I look into his face, and I'm not sure he's really ours. Will he ever smile back when I look at him? Will he know I'm his mother? What will we do to make sure he can take care of himself?"

Soon enough, Mom and Dad recovered from their initial shock. They summoned the experts, and my life and theirs began to fall into a workable rhythm. The teachers made sure my parents knew how to raise me. I learned how to crawl, walk, recognize their voices, and to take care of myself as I grew.

The years went by, I went to school where—much to my parents' relief—I became a good student. This gave my dad the grist he needed to begin seriously thinking about my future.

One day, he had an idea. "You're never going to make money," he declared, "unless you become a lawyer. Look at those teachers who've tried to help you all these years. Do you think they make a lot of money? Besides," he observed, "they've been very little help to you, rotating in and out of your life every time they have to report for military duty." The mantra that guided his plan was simple: "Get your education and make something of yourself."

Getting my education wasn't as easy as he thought. Because of the war, the high school I attended was built like a fortress. Security guards were stationed at the entrances, and many of the teachers wore military uniforms. The school was laid out labyrinthine, so during the long trek from class to class, there was plenty of opportunity for taunting and pranks. It was during these pilgrimages that I learned just how abnormal I was.

It turned out that a few years after I was born, and the war had broken out, many of the kids had benefited—if you could call it that—from a new law that made it mandatory for all newly conceived children to receive dual programming. Their initial infusion came during genetic prescreening at the time of their conception. This service was made available to any pregnant mother who sought medical care. My parents had foregone this procedure.

Then for those who could afford treatment, doctors took additional steps to ensure that as few of them as possible gave birth to children with "deficiencies." Pregnant mothers and their fetuses could undergo genetic engineering to prevent "defects." Lest this be construed as humanitarian, the not-so-hidden motive for making these services available was the preparation of healthy children to become soldiers.

Thus, there developed an "underground" movement of parents who subscribed to the "natural" approach and managed to avoid the screening and engineering process. Many were peace-loving people who did not want their children "bred" to be soldiers.

As I hit my adolescence, I realized that almost everyone received a third round of programming, a liberal dose of intolerance. This round, provided by society, meted out much prejudice against anyone who couldn't hold his own. Somewhere along the way, the social order had insidiously shifted from "kind and gentle" to "sink or swim." The prejudice came from an understandable source—fear. After all, the country was at war.

"Look at the blind boy." The jeer would have been bad enough coming from the class bully, but this particular barb was thrust by one of the class intellectuals. "His genes must not be very good if this is what happened to him."

"Leave him alone," one of the girls, who had a soft spot for me, said, "It's not his fault."

When I told my father that the kids teased me, and the girls spurned me, he said, "You'll get a better job than any of those kids, and then we'll see who has the last laugh."

It might not be my fault, I thought. *But there's no escaping it, I don't fit in.* With so many social encounters resulting in strife, I grew reluctant to interact with my peers. This only served to make it even harder to get along when I did interact with them. I even gave up on having a date for the senior prom. Instead of dancing the night away, I sat at home, listening to a ball game with my father.

My dad tried to console me. "There's nothing like a ball game to make you forget about your troubles."

Reluctantly I took the bait. "You're right. Baseball is a great sport. I'd be a ballplayer if I could."

"I'll bet you'd be pretty good too," he said. My father was always encouraging in that way. "You'd certainly play hard."

Dad had done his best to teach me everything he knew about the game. He set up a batting tee and taught me to switch hit. I grew quite fond of smashing a ball into a net set up several feet away. I'd hit a small pail full of balls into the net, retrieve them, and start again. I spent hours at this endeavor on weekends, conjuring make-believe games in my head and narrating the action much as I heard the radio broadcasters do while lying in bed at night. I loved baseball more than anything else. It saddened me that I couldn't follow this dream to reality.

Following my father's advice, I concentrated on my studies and got into a good college. As soon as I moved into the dorm, I found out that having neglected my social life was as handicapping as being unable to see. I didn't know, for example, how to compete for the attention of the coeds.

Failing at this aspect of campus life was frustrating. When I tried asking women on dates, I received polite refusals. "I'm sure you are very nice" was the typical reply. "But I'm not dating right now."

My manhood, thus, diminished. I retreated to the comfort of my room and a good ballgame.

The hurt wedged into a corner of my spirit and wouldn't let go. Deprivation led to sexual frustration. I dreamed of being like some of the guys in my dorm—seemingly able to land a different girl every week. Many lonely dormitory weekends passed. I vowed that if I ever could figure out how to do it, I'd someday play the field, if not with a baseball, then with women.

A vague awareness crept in. I was depressed. It wasn't the kind of depression that relegates one to his bed, unable to eat or sleep, but more the dysphoria that comes from being unable to solve one's problems. It was the feeling of gloom that envelopes one when he feels inefficacious in matters of importance. This led me down a new career path. I decided to major in, what else, psychology.

One day, I just had to let it out. Complaining to my roommate, I blurted, "Everything is so hard. I'm sick of having to deal with people shying away from me. I'm tired of the simplest things being a struggle. I can't even read a book or ask a girl for a date without expending large amounts of energy. If I could see, things would be a lot easier."

He shot back, "You call yourself a psychology major. Heal thyself, doctor."

My roommate had stunned me. He said, "You have a choice. You can become a lawyer and sue your way through life, or you can learn more about human nature and decipher the mysteries of coping in an imperfect world."

The study of human nature proved fascinating. With "inside knowledge," I began to feel I understood people better. My self-confidence rose. I felt more in tune with the people around me, even managing to meet a nice girl, Cheryl. We became a steady couple.

The time finally came to decide on a career. "I'm never going to be as good as I can be so long as I'm dragged down by not being able to see," I said during a long discussion with Cheryl. "I might as well do something I'm naturally suited for, like counseling the blind."

"Sounds good to me," she answered. "At least you have an advantage in knowing what it's like."

With little additional thought, I took an advanced degree and went straight to work. Cheryl became an accountant and found a position with the local bank.

My days blurred into one. They began with a bus ride to the office and a review of my cases. A talking computerized system worked well for this task. Taxis ferried me around town to visit my clients. My job required me to see several of them daily, and the public transport system, which had been allowed to deteriorate, was quite inadequate to the task of getting someone from one side of the city to another and back within a few hours. This was too bad as the self-driving automobile program was on the verge of being rolled out when the economy switched to a war footing.

I took pride in my job, carrying the largest caseload in the office and helping more people than anyone else on my team obtain the few jobs available in the city. The economy was not only in tatters, but a survivalist mentality had taken hold. The best jobs were those controlled by the military. Anyone who enlisted had special advantage. Everyone else competed fiercely for the civilian jobs like the one I held. Those who couldn't compete sat home on the dole.

"Why don't you take the promotional exam," my boss asked. "You're ready for the next step."

"I guess so," I answered. "Do you really think they'd give me a senior position if I did well?" I feared I'd be given the same treatment others not qualified to serve in the military had received, being overlooked for positions of authority.

"You won't have a chance if you don't try," he answered.

During the test, I wasted an inordinate amount of time fruitlessly trying to figure out how to use the computerized reading tablet they provided. This only compounded the difficulty I faced trying to interpret the data charts critical to answering many of the arcane questions on the test.

"These tablets are confusing," I told the volunteer assigned to me. "Can't you help me figure out how to use this thing?"

The volunteer, a young woman on assignment from the military, demurred. "You should be able to handle this yourself," she stated matter-of-factly. "If you're going to move up in the ranks," she added, "you'd better figure out how to rise above these obstacles."

"This isn't a fair fight," I shot back. "By the way," I added, "I thought you were here to help me, and here you are, refusing to cover my back."

"Sorry," she replied. "I'm not authorized to help you by doing the test for you."

"You are supposed to help make it a level playing field, so I have a fighting chance of showing what I know."

She had no words of comfort for me.

Finishing the exam as best I could, I exited the testing room demoralized, convinced I had blown my chances for advancement.

"So much for progress in information access," I cursed under my breath as I headed home on the bus. "I feel like so much excrement, and I'll be damned if there's anything I can do about it."

I must have been talking louder than I thought because the man across the aisle piped up. "Hey, my man, you look like you've been put through the ringer."

"Yeah," I blurted. "I just got screwed over taking a promotional exam."

"Too bad," he answered. "If it were me," he suggested, "I'd get ripped and then get laid."

Thus, I dropped into my favorite bar to drown my sorrows. Getting off before reaching my usual stop, and with head and spirits drooping, I limped into the watering hole.

On previous occasions, when I'd felt down in the dumps, this establishment had become a source of friendship and solace. The place lay only a few blocks from my apartment complex. I enjoyed going there because if I got blitzed, it was a no-brainer to get home.

The bar was a three-sided affair ringed with high stools. After experimenting with, or should I say, stumbling to all parts of the bar, my favorite drinking station became a stool strategically positioned near the bartender so he could keep an eye on my glass, refilling it when it got low. Tables were scattered around the sawdust-covered floor between the entrance and my barstool. I had to zigzag my way with skillful use of my cane to get to the bar. The bartender told me they kept the lights low to attract women inclined toward romance. The music ranged from sultry jazz to rock that might promote hard dancing.

"What'll it be?" the bartender asked. He politely waited for me to say, "The usual," and then he slid the pale ale he'd already poured in front of me.

"You look like hell." He observed. "What's up? Broke up with your girl?"

"No," I mumbled. "I just blew a promotional exam."

"That's too bad," he answered. "What do you think went wrong?"

Just then, a bevy of women sauntered into the bar. Given their banter and loudness, they would—under normal circumstances—have impressed me as fun-loving. When my interest didn't perk up as it usually did, the barkeep took notice.

"Wow," he commented. "Those girls are a lively bunch, and you're not even paying attention. You really are feeling low."

I explained what had gone wrong during the exam, complained about life in general, and slugged down my ale. The bartender quickly refilled my glass.

"Wait until the results come back." He tried to comfort. "You may be surprised."

"There's no use in trying," I cried in my beer. "It feels like walking through quicksand every time I attempt to do something new and different."

The women giggled and chattered among themselves. I thought, *Maybe I'll pick up one of them and go salvage my masculinity.*

Listening carefully to their conversations, it was difficult to tell whether any of them was looking around for a pickup. Then I thought, *What would I do if I thought one of them was interested? Just walk boldly up to her and ask if I could buy her a drink? Fat chance, she'd say yes.*

The bartender sensed my need to salvage some self-respect. He asked, "Do you want to buy one of those girls a drink? I can tell you which one seems most promising."

"No," I answered. If I cheated on my girlfriend, I'd probably get caught. If I didn't get caught, I mused. I'd probably hate myself and feel so guilty. I'd give myself away.

Still, I couldn't help imagining what it might be like to have a quick frolic. I wanted to try, but for the moment, I was too afraid to risk another defeat.

"Damn it," I muttered. "It's probably for the best anyway." I gave up the fantasy, paid the bartender, and slipped into the autumn night.

I walked homeward. "If I could only see a little bit," I said to no one. Scolding myself, I said, "Ah, you're drunk. There's no point to wishing for something you can't have." A thought poked into consciousness: "Or is there?"

As I walked, the cold air cleared my head. My thinking sharpened, and the epiphany hit me. *If I could have seen the charts and graphs on that exam for just a few seconds, I would have done well on that promotional exam.* My next thought made me chuckle. *If I had been able to look at those girls and walk up to them, I might have been able to pick up one of them.*

Struck by my epiphany about the exam and giddy at my self-diagnosed genius, I walked right past the gate to my apartment complex. The guard called me back to reality. He said, "I see you've been carousing. Punch in your code, and I'll let you in. If you're too inebriated to do so, I'd suggest you sober up, or you are going to be frosting up out there."

I punched in my security code and scrambled through the gate before it could hit me in the behind.

I arrived at my apartment. Skipping my tradition of removing shoes and standing my cane in its usual place, I went straight to my electronic diary and recorded the following:

"It has occurred to me today that it may never be possible, so long as the war continues, for sufficient scientific resources to be devoted to the task of providing sight to people who have never seen. So much technology is devoted to security that I doubt if anyone would devote the resources to something that could only benefit a small minority of our population. However, I wonder if this technology could provide us with high-quality vision for just short periods of time. Being able to see for, say, a few minutes at a time would be incredibly useful for people accustomed to functioning without any sight at all. If only there was a way, I'd be on the top of the list. If I had fifteen minutes of eyesight a day, I'd have my fifteen minutes of fame." I quipped into my notebook.

I put a query out on the electronic net. "Does anyone know of new research to provide sight to the blind?"

CHAPTER 2

Boundaries of Fear

The war began about a fifth of the way into the millennium. Although my friends and I were only high school students, we immediately began wondering whether it wasn't time to start protesting.

We worried about the paranoia that zealous leaders can conjure in the minds of a deliberately misinformed and frightened public. We'd just completed a unit in history class about late twentieth and early twenty-first century wars in Southeast Asia, the Middle East, Africa, South Asia, and spot wars nearly everywhere else. Full of the promise of the power of the citizenry to affect political decisions, we listened with consternation as every day, the news broadcasted reports of fighter planes bombing terrorist targets. They ranged from those which had destructively attacked our country to targets of concern about future danger, reports of which seemed to crop up every day.

"It seems that we managed to alienate ourselves from everyone back then." I shrugged.

"Yep, everyone wanted a piece of us," my history teacher commented.

"Why did they bomb two of our most important buildings on 9/11?" a girl asked.

"Because they thought we were hoarding all the wealth, and that they were poor because of our lavish and immoral lifestyle," a classmate answered.

"So we got revenge on them, and then they got revenge back upon us," she countered. Her face was red with the anger these conversations always seemed to rouse.

"Today's news is full of civil wars and regional conflicts breaking out around the world and usually both mixed together," our teacher added. "The attacks are not just targeted at us."

"Why did we have to send troops to all those countries?" I asked. "In the past twenty years, we've tried to kick ass in two different places on the other side of the world and ended up leaving a bigger mess there than when we started."

"In the long run," our teacher opined, "a nation-building strategy won't work. There are too many factions, and even if you could tell your friend from your enemy, the situation would change before you knew it. Now we have external and internal terrorism, and that is why we are in this predicament."

The evening news grew more dismal. "Look at that," my father grumbled. "The luxury tax has just moved to double digits. They are wasting too much money on fighting a so-called war that can never be won."

"What do you mean it can never be won?" I asked. Over the months since the fighting had escalated, I'd grown more and more frightened of what might happen to our country if the fighting continued.

"We're either going to need more troops and weapons, or we're going to have to figure out how to end this mess," my father answered. "Just look what's happening to us. There is a technology freeze. Nonessential manufacturing is on hold. Spin-off technologies are no longer trickling to the populous. We can't even get equipment for you to use in school."

A subtle effect was occurring to everyday civil rights. People were becoming afraid to discuss matters contrary to the current order. "Don't talk about the president or the military in anything but respectful terms," my mother implored.

"What will happen?" I asked.

"Nothing you can put your finger on," she answered, "but I've heard of people being refused bank loans when they should have been given them. There are even rumors that people who have spoken out against the war have been denied promotions or had their businesses torched. And where have all the liberal newspapers gone?"

"What does this have to do with me? I'm just a kid."

"Your dad and I wouldn't want you to risk losing out on a scholarship or the opportunity to get into a good college," she explained. "It's better to just go about your business quietly and don't give anybody reason to make life more difficult for you than it already is."

Everywhere one turned, police and national guard units could be seen at positions guarding buildings and bridges. Air and sea travel became a fearful endeavor. Military forces were deployed to guard the "defender nation's" respective perimeters, and soldiers were sent to various hot spots around the world as part of multinational operations.

At home, it was almost the same thing. Border walls were everywhere, not just between our country and those adjacent but around all large cities and towns. Life in rural places was like the American Wild West: every man and woman for themselves.

"Can anyone give me an example of civilizations that have fallen from dominance?" our history teacher asked.

"Why should we think about that?" a boy retorted. "This is a modern history class."

"Can anyone answer that question?"

After no one spoke, the teacher asked if we'd ever heard of George Santayana.

"Yes," a few of us answered.

"Of what did old George admonish?"

"He said those who don't remember the past are condemned to repeat it," I volunteered.

"That is indeed what he is most remembered for," my teacher replied. Then he went on.

"Did you know that George Santayana was born in Spain and lived most of his life in America? He was not only an historian but also a philosopher and writer. Old George never lost sight of his global roots. He looked at American and other cultures from a broad perspective. In fact, he even wrote a critique of German philosophy way back in 1915. Perhaps if we had listened to him," my teacher speculated, "we might have avoided World War II."

The class was getting restless with all this talk about the distant past. "What did he say about American culture?" a girl piped up.

"Old George said that Americans, lacking the time to live in the mind, use quantity as a justification for lack of quality in their achievements."

"So what? We only live once. Why shouldn't we get as much out of life as we can, especially when many of the luxuries of life are so scarce?"

This challenge came not from one of us but from a teacher who just happened to be passing the open door of our classroom.

Surprised, our teacher turned and stared. "Mr. Smith, don't you believe that we have succumbed to a habit in this country of trying to accumulate material goods at the expense of quality of life?"

"Perhaps so," Mr. Smith answered. "But what else would you have us do?"

The girl next to me spoke up, "Maybe if we were a little less selfish, we wouldn't be in the mess we're in now."

"Now I understand why you asked about other civilizations," I rejoined. "They all overextended themselves, probably for the sake of wealth and power, and they all fell. Rome, Germany, and now maybe us."

"So let's turn to today's lesson, the upcoming presidential election. What are the issues?"

"The war, of course," chanted the class in unison.

"Yes," Mr. Smith replied. He had joined the discussion, and our teacher didn't seem to mind. "However, I'm sure you will agree there is a bigger issue. What might that be?"

Our teacher jumped in. "Yes, on the surface, the issue will be the wars. But underneath, there is something more troublesome. Perhaps this excerpt from today's paper will help." He read. "The challengers warn that fighting multiple micro-wars is not the answer. They campaign wherever possible on a platform that the risk of global war must be mitigated by new geopolitical policies that share the wealth of nations and demonstrate mutual respect for the welfare of all people. The continued domination of the rich and powerful in our own country they admonish can only lead to extreme consequences." He looked up. Seeing our attention glued upon his words and confusion upon our faces, he challenged. "Well, what does this mean?"

I attempted an answer, "I guess it means we have a choice. Either continue the way we are and doom ourselves to constant fighting or change our basic ways."

"That's the issue. Can we realistically expect to do that?"

In the short run, I guess the answer was no. The election came and went. Although the challengers may have been right, the fears of the people prevented fast action. The reform movement went down to defeat. In fact, making peace was never seriously discussed because the "defender nations" truly believed the "enemy" was motivated by unfounded rage and jealousy.

Having been given another four years to carry out his agenda, the newly reelected president stated, "'These attacks are incursions on freedom.' The heads of the military were gathered for a major strategy-setting session. 'They are motivated by paranoia and years of programming young Third World people for suicide bombings and continuous warfare. They have convinced their martyrs that they have nothing to lose by inflicting a reign of terror upon the rest of the world.' And most telling, 'We must prosecute our overseas and domestic battles with utmost rigor, using every piece of technology at our disposal.'"

The military was reorganized. The impetus for this momentous change was perhaps the two most seminal technologies to come along in a century, the electromagnetic force field and genetic engineering.

"With powerful emitters, positioned at specific intervals around the entire country, the borders are now hermetically sealed," the anchor man on the evening news reported. "Countries, cities, and towns possessing the shield are now able to effectively protect themselves from outside intrusion."

"Great news!" my father announced. "As much as it turns my stomach that it's come to this," he said, "I guess it's better we're inside the shield than out there."

"Hush," my mother scolded. "You know this is tantamount to burying our heads in the sand."

"I know," he replied. Turning to me, he asked, "What do you think, son?"

"My history teacher has gotten us to look at this whole state of affairs from a broader perspective," I answered. "I think we've gotten ourselves into a fine mess, and I hope we figure out how to live in peace with the whole world someday."

"That's a good philosophy," my parents admitted. Then our attention was drawn back to the news.

"The Defense Shield Force will ensure that we and our allies can continue to live our everyday lives in relative security," the chairman of the Joint Chiefs declared. He was standing at a podium before the graduating class at West Point. "You will lead the way in guarding our homeland," he continued. "The basic mission is the same now as it has been since the inception of our great nation—the defense of freedom and the way of life we have made for ourselves in this great land."

Then in answer to critics who accused the military of merely hunkering down to wait for the enemy to come to them rather than "taking it to the enemy" as had always been the approach, the chairman said, "You will guard all land passages between us and our friends and between us and our enemies. No one in our society will starve or live with the privations that would occur without the corridors you will keep safe. No one need fear leaving their homes because you will be there to make certain those who would destroy us are kept well at arm's length. Your willingness to place yourself in harm's way for the benefit of all humanity is a calling beyond reproach, beyond our ability to ever fully repay you."

My high school graduation ceremony was punctuated by a keynote speech from the leading physicist of the day. Along with a Herculean effort from hundreds of scientists, engineers, and energy specialists, the man who stood before us had accomplished the hitherto impossible.

"Creating the shield had to be delayed until it was possible to take advantage of the immense power generated by controlled fusion reactors," he said. "Our scientists used the processing power of mega-computers and the elegance of finely controlled superhot micro-lasers to harness the power of hydrogen atoms for the benefit of humanity."

Then he shifted gears. "Nearly all of you have been prepared since before you were born for the greatest duty a society can offer you, the job of defending our people with your strength and intelligence. You have been bred to be citizens, parents, productive workers, and most of all, soldiers. You should be proud to be graduating today and ready to take your place both at the guard post and in the universities."

We sat in the bleachers, listening to the speech. "He sure sounds proud of himself," the girl from my history class leaned over and whispered.

"Shh!" I exhorted. "I'm fascinated by this stuff."

"Don't let it go to your head," she admonished. "Think about what we learned in class and consider the implications."

The Shield was impregnable. Missiles attempting to penetrate it detonated on contact. Bullets melted. Chemical compounds dissociated. Living things couldn't get within a millimeter of the field before whatever semblance of a nervous system caused them to back off or have their cells fried.

I return to the dream. Am I here? Am I there? I float in and out of consciousness, and I see a life. Is this my life? Or does it belong to another? I float off, once again leaving the sounds of medical equipment behind.

CHAPTER 3

Joe

Joe attended the same university as I did. I studied psychology; he participated in athletics and drove himself toward a degree in engineering. I was working part time in the counseling center when he decided to drop in.

Joe was admittedly hot-blooded and had been that way ever since he could remember. Deciding to temper his personality, he signed up for weekly counseling sessions.

"I've got a blind fellow for you," my supervisor announced at the morning staff meeting. "He has requested help with anger management. Can you relate?"

"I'll say," I blurted. "But don't you think perhaps you've stereotyped us? Why give him to me? Just because I'm blind?"

"I admit," he explained. "I have made a few assumptions based on what I perceive to be your ability to understand his world as a blind person. Beyond that," he continued, "I think you will grow as much from this peer-counseling experience as he will."

Sure enough, Joe and I had shared many of the same experiences. It turned out to be surprisingly easy for us to talk about our respective anger mismanagement. I told Joe how frustration led me to feeling depressed; he told me how frustration led him to pugnacity. He promised to try to get me to be more assertive; I promised to try to teach him, if not how to keep calm, then at least how to refrain from punching someone.

We hit it off nicely. Although we were only partially successful in helping each other eliminate anger from our lives, the anger that remained would contribute to our greatest adventure together.

By the time the embryo Joe was conceived, preliminary tests on a new method of soldier building had borne fruit. Several babies had been cloned from the cells of prominent soldiers, including Joe's parents. Time would tell if they would grow into equally skillful fighting men and women, but Joe's was the last cohort to be conceived under the program.

The new shield defense system provided a better solution. Universal soldier production was no longer needed to thwart the enemy. This was fortunate since avoidance of the program was mounting, much like most involuntary population-control methods had in the past.

Before they changed the rules, there was one notable failure. The parents were a professional infantryman and a woman fighter pilot. The father (who commanded a tank battalion that patrolled the border) provided the cells that were cloned, and the mother carried the child to term. The boy that emerged was a near-perfect duplicate of his father—younger, of course, and inexplicably unable to see.

As he grew, the boy appeared to have inherited all the faculties of his father, except that he had a hot temper. Although lack of sight might prevent him from becoming either a grunt or flyboy, he, nonetheless, developed into a strong and agile adolescent, one worthy of consideration for a career in the military if circumstances had been different.

Joe readily absorbed both his parents' interests. He badgered his father into teaching him how to shoot, even if he couldn't see his targets, and asked him to let him ride in a tank. There at an early age, Joe learned that powerful machines are guided by computers and other fancy equipment. "If I could work these gadgets," he surmised, "I could drive a tank."

"I'll bet you could," his father quipped. He hadn't taken Joe's pronouncement as anything more than a boy's fantasy. Joe, on the other hand, took his father's lighthearted answer as an endorsement.

Joe had an even more abiding respect for his mother's profession. He nagged her to take him flying. Feeling the thrust of the engines as his mother jerked the plane into the air and the tilt of the fighter plane as she banked first one way and then another and recovering from the terror of precipitous falling when she placed the craft into a dive, Joe was hooked. He knew after a single flight that he wanted to fly more than anything else.

Joe realized he would have to be in superb physical condition to handle the rigors of piloting an aircraft. When he turned twelve, he signed up for school sports. By the time he was in high school, he had become a well-regarded wrestler, weight lifter, and swimmer. Because he also realized the need for school smarts to operate the sophisticated computers and other equipment in the cockpit, Joe buckled down and achieved good grades, especially in math and science.

Unfortunately, his tolerance for frustration was quite low. He got angry when he didn't score perfectly on school exams and was fit to be tied when he lost a match or race. On numerous occasions, Joe's parents were called to the principal's office where they found him detained for having gotten into a fight.

"We've got to stop this, Joe," the principal admonished. "Any more fighting, and I'll suspend you from athletic competition."

It was no wonder Joe relied upon physical prowess to settle disputes. He'd grown up surrounded by physicality. From the time he could walk, his father placed him on stationary bicycles and weight machines. His mother filled his head with stories of high and low-level flight. He loved being strapped into simulators where he could manipulate the controls and pretend to operate either a tank or fighter plane. This further fueled his fantasies. These tools, Joe realized, could conquer the enemy. And to Joe, anyone or anything that halted his progress was the enemy.

Not long after his first flight, Joe decided he wanted to be an astronaut. Dreaming that someday he would be the first blind person to venture into space, he devoured books on astronomy and made sure he understood trigonometry and physics.

"If I trace this parabola," Joe explained one evening during dinner, "I can imagine how the 'vomit comet' simulates weightlessness. On the rapid descent," he continued, oblivious to his parents' smiles of admiration, "occupants of the plane can drift around the cabin to their heart's content."

"Or," his mother quipped, "until they get sick to their stomachs and barf."

"That wouldn't happen to me," Joe asserted. "I've been in enough simulators to know I can take anything air or even space travel can dish out."

Rambling on, he continued, "I remember how scared I was the first time you dived a plane with me in it, Mom. Now I love it."

"Alas," his mother told him when it became obvious where Joe's aspirations lay, "You might not be able to be a pilot or astronaut." She saw the pain spread across Joe's face.

"What do you mean? I want to fly more than anything in the world."

Shifting restlessly, she admitted, "I mean I can't see how it will ever be possible for you to absorb all the visual information you will need during actual flight."

Joe's temper began to rise. His face flushed as he stood up and prepared to storm from the room.

Placing his hands on hips in a defiant stance, he whirled and moved toward the door. He hadn't taken more than a couple steps when he ran straight into a bear hug.

His father, having just walked into the room, corralled his charging bull of a son and, with powerful arms, held him tight. Joe wanted to fight, but because his father's massive arms were a force to be reckoned with, he immediately desisted.

"Now, Joe, calm down," his father ordered. "There are plenty of things you can do for the cause. We can't function out there on the line without technology, you know." Then in a tactical shift designed to turn Joe's head around, he continued, "I'll bet Mom and I can give you enough information to make you the best tank or aircraft designer this country ever had. All you have to do is study hard and get a college diploma. I'll bet if you get a degree in computer design, you'll knock them dead. You can do it, son."

Joe's mother joined them at the center of the room. Attempting to comfort him, she placed a hand on his shoulder and looked directly into his face. "You already have a good idea what your Dad and I do for a living," she said. "This can work to your advantage. You don't have to give up your dreams, Joe." Then she urged, "Just tone them down a bit."

The advice stuck. Joe quietly calculated. He could earn a respectable living, contribute to the cause, and keeping this part to himself, follow his star. *Somehow*, he thought, *I will fly*.

Joe channeled his talents into aeronautical engineering. Luckily because he entered school before funding for tactile graphics production had been cut off, he had the tools he needed to keep up with his classmates. Had Joe begun his training only a few years later, the equipment that faithfully reproduced his graphs and charts and enabled him to handle complex mathematical equations would have been withdrawn from the classrooms and converted into parts for the military machine.

Joe graduated with honors and quickly found work as a civilian aircraft designer in the Air Defense Shield. Working now for the same organization as his mother, he helped develop the latest schematics for stealthy space plane technology. In his spare time, he reset his sights on flying solo.

Enlisting the help of his coworkers, he set about designing a lighter-than-air craft that he could fly on his own. Joe's friends were dubious until he showed them his plans. They called for a highly stable wing system that would hold the craft aloft longer in the face of diminishing winds than conventional lighter-than-aircrafts of their time.

Joe hoped the design would buy him the time he might need to figure out, through auditory feedback from special instruments he also designed, how to recover from loss of updraft. Impressed again with Joe's concepts, his friends eagerly helped him bring the machine into reality.

Joe's best friend, Jim, a flight instructor and pilot, successfully test-flew the craft. Now if Joe could only figure out how to fly by himself, all would be right with the world.

Jim and his ground crew placed beacons on the ground in strategic places near landing zones. The beacons up linked to cockpit instruments that enunciated their position relative to the aircraft. A lightweight radar system and radio equipment completed the panoply of tools Joe hoped would "talk" him through the maneuvers he would have to make to keep his craft above the proper wind currents, navigate, and safely land.

Joe spent countless hours in a simulator to prepare for his test flight. Learning how to steer and judge wind currents proved quite difficult.

"You've lost the current again," Jim barked. "What do you hear those instruments telling you?"

After hours of trying, Jim came to a difficult conclusion, "Ultimately, Joe, you won't be able to pilot this alone if you can't see what's in front of you and below."

Joe couldn't accept this. "Can't you talk me through the key maneuvers by radio?" He pressed. "If you can get me into the proper currents, I know I can maneuver just fine. Then when I need to land, if my beacons and radar fail me, you can talk me back."

"No, it's too complicated. In fact, every flight instructor I've spoken to insists it's suicidal. Just to make sure," his best friend said, "I've already tried it myself. The instruments are not sufficiently verbal for me to make sense of the auditory output. That system was designed to be used in combination with vision, not instead of it."

"I could figure out how to make sense of the output," Joe insisted.

"You would have to have such fast reaction time," Jim went on, "By the time you decipher the signals or get an instruction from me on the ground, the currents will have already changed to the point that, even with your brilliantly designed wing system, the plane just won't stay aloft. Sorry, Joe, I'm afraid I couldn't sanction you for solo flight."

Temper flaring, Joe headed home. Always the athlete, Joe considered the art of safe travel for a blind person not unlike a sports event. It took agility, strength, good sensory ability, and good reflexes to move quickly. Laser enhancements to his cane enabled him to walk swiftly. This, in turn, gave him the punch he needed to defy anyone who might cross his path. On this day, Joe was in no mood to be slowed down. Therefore, when someone collided with him, Joe had a bad reaction.

"Watch where you're going," the man growled.

Joe wheeled and said, "You watch out. I was walking straight. Didn't you see me?"

"Listen you, blind bastard," the man shot back, "you people have a chip on your shoulder. You think the world owes you something. Well, I'm here to tell you we don't."

"What the hell are you talking about?" He was ready to face off against the stranger, but remembering our many anger management conversations, he reconsidered. Turning away, he muttered, "Never mind."

He resumed his trip homeward. "I don't have time for your bullshit," he said, calling over his shoulder.

Joe had taken only a few steps when the man said in a voice so loud it seemed to him the entire neighborhood could hear, "You blind people are an abomination. They should have euthanized you monsters straight from the womb."

Joe reacted swiftly. Stepping within a few inches of the man, he struck out with an overhand right. The punch landed squarely in the center of the man's face and rocked him back. Because Joe had tried a little boxing while in college and was not unused to the shock of hitting a man in the face, he knew he'd done damage. Anticipating a return punch, Joe automatically recoiled and protected his face with one arm and his stomach with the other. To guard against a kick, he turned slightly sideways.

The man stepped toward Joe. Failing to think that if he were to approach stealthily, Joe might not be able to discern his exact location or intent; he moved predictably and noisily. Joe picked up on the time and angle of his approach. The man jabbed directly for Joe's midsection. Joe easily parried the body blow and shoved the man away from him.

It was now clear to Joe that he had much more strength than his nemesis. He moved in for the kill. Stepping into the space vacated by the man as he staggered backward, Joe swiped with a sword swing of his cane. He struck the man across the neck. Caught by surprise by the aggressive assault, the man yelped in pain and surprise. Clutching his throat, the man gasped for the breath Joe had just knocked out of him.

Having ascertained the man's exact location, Joe dropped the cane and lunged. Grabbing him around the waist, Joe lifted the man into the air and slammed him to the ground. He heard a sickening crack and felt the man go limp. Shaken, Joe berated himself for his behavior. "I shouldn't have done that," he said to himself. He bent low and listened for signs of life.

Hearing the man's rasping breath, relieved he hadn't killed the guy, and sensing no other movement coming from him, Joe assumed that the man had been knocked unconscious.

"Damn!" he muttered.

"What have I done now?" Retrieving his cane, Joe quickly walked away.

Pulling out his communicator tablet, he called the police and requested help for his vanquished foe. The police took Joe's report and saw to it the man was taken to the hospital. "We won't charge you with assault just yet," the officer told Joe. "While we wait to get the other fellow's side of the story, just keep your nose clean."

My phone rang. It was Joe. He told me what happened. Since graduating, Joe and I had stayed in touch. No longer his counselor and not wishing to practice amateur psychology, I sympathized, "I'd have done the same thing if I thought I could fight," I admitted. "As it is," I concluded, "my inability to punch my way out of a paper bag would have forced me to suck it up. Then I'd probably be fuming for weeks."

"I'm not fuming," Joe admitted. "I got it all out of my system."

"So what's wrong?"

"I could have killed that guy," Joe croaked. "It scared me. I don't know my own strength, and I guess I still haven't learned how to control my anger."

"Have you told your folks about this?"

"I'm going to do that now," Joe promised.

After relating to his father what had happened, Joe speculated, "I'll bet lots of people think the same thing about me as that guy. They're just afraid to say it."

"No, Joe," his father attempted. "Most people are much more humane and a lot smarter."

"I can tell people think of me as a freak," Joe continued. "They always act nervous when I approach. Then because they are nervous, they act stupid. It makes me feel angry."

"You feel angry because you feel alone," his mother offered. She had just entered the room. "Just remember," she added, "we love you."

"You are going to have to do something about that temper of yours," his father said. "It's one thing to have the muscle to punch someone's lights out, it's another thing to use that brawn wisely. Restraint takes a lot more strength than fighting."

"Is that what they taught you in the military?" Joe spat out. "I don't think so."

"It's what this country should have learned a long time ago," his father responded. "We wouldn't be living behind a shield now if we'd just had a little more respect for those in the world less fortunate than us."

Joe skipped dinner and crawled straight into bed. He wanted to cry. "Why does life have to be so miserable? Isn't it hard enough to hold on to your dreams because of all the obstacles we face without people wishing you didn't even exist to begin with?"

The shock of his pugilistic encounter dissipated, but the disruption to Joe's spirits did not. Using a tried and true antidote, he settled into bed and resorted to musing about flying. "I guess I'm either going to have to find people who can help me, or I'm going to have to find some other way to fly."

Rolling onto his side, Joe winced. He'd pulled a few muscles picking up and slamming his assailant. Groaning, he said, "I've got to do some martial arts training."

Imagining what it would be like to be an astronaut and fly into outer space had always worked to mitigate his cares and woes. But tonight, his musings were supplanted by intrusive thoughts of the messages he had absorbed from the assailant, Jim, and his mother: "You can't do it."

Anger seized him again. Joe sat up. "I won't give up on this idea. I can't stand the thought that people can treat me like shit one minute, say I can't have my dreams in another, and yet tell me how lucky I am to have accomplished as much as I have."

Finally calming his nerves, Joe allowed sleep to overtake him. The night was quiet for a change. No military flyovers disturbed the peace; no alerts permeated the evening news causing the citizenry to experience a collective adrenalin rush. The air was cool and crisp—a perfect night for sleeping and dreaming.

CHAPTER 4

Good Dreams, Bad Dreams

She crawled into bed and snuggled close. I felt her hot breath in my ear. "I saw you at the bar and just had to follow you home."

"Who are you?" I asked. I could scarcely believe my good fortune. Not only was the woman in bed with me, she had completely disrobed and had begun exercising several options stored in her love-making repertoire.

"I'm the girl you asked the bartender about. Don't you remember?"

"Oh yes." I laughed. "You sure sounded sexy, and now I see you really are."

"Well, let's see what we can do." With that, she began rhythmically moving her body against mine.

I grew aroused and began to reciprocate.

The phone rang. I awoke with a start. It was after midnight. There was no one in bed with me. All I had to show for my amorous encounter was an unresolved sexual tension that left me throbbing with unfulfilled need. "Who the heck can that be?" I muttered.

It was Joe again. "What is it, Joe?" I managed to spit out between quasi-orgasmic gasps for air.

"I just had the worst nightmare," he whispered. "I don't know what it means, but I just had to call and let you know about it."

"You just interrupted the closest thing to a wet dream I've ever had."

"Sorry, man, you'd better get together with Cheryl as soon as possible."

"Very funny," I replied. "What's wrong anyway? Why are you calling me at this hour?"

Joe hesitated, uncertain whether to annoy me further with what he was beginning to think might be a childish need to express his fears. Finally, the pressure of his distress got the better of him. "I dreamed I was flying in space. It's something I've always wanted to do."

"So…" I said, trying to hide the irritation I was feeling about my aborted dream.

"I've always thought that it'd be full of joy and adventure, and instead it scared me to death."

"What happened?"

"Nothing. There was absolute silence, and I couldn't do anything but force myself to wake up."

"You couldn't hear or feel anything?" I probed.

"No, I experienced nothing at all. I kept asking myself, 'What happened to the G-forces from the launch? Why don't I feel weightless? Where is everyone?'"

"Then what happened?"

Joe pondered. "I was really scared, more scared than I've ever been. Maybe this is a sign that flying is just a pipe dream."

"Maybe it's the aftereffect of that fight you had earlier this evening." I was wide awake now; the resentment of having been torn away from my sexy encounter had waned.

"Perhaps the only way to never be afraid is to be able to see," Joe said.

His non sequitur would take some connecting of the dots for me to arrive at the place Joe had landed. I thought about it, and may have been about to make the connection when Joe spoke again. "I wonder if there actually might be a way for us to see."

I recalled the young woman who in my dream had just crawled into bed with me and then poof, disappeared. I thought about other more serious hardships I'd endured. Although they may have not quite reached the level of severity of what Joe had just gone through, I began feeling sorry for myself again. Tears welled up in my eyes. Now two of us, feeling badly together, were itching for a solution. It was time for action.

"Joe," I replied slowly and in a low and ominous tone, "call me in the morning, about eight o'clock. I'd like to discuss what you have in mind." And when we connected at the appointed time, we placed a call that would forever change our lives.

CHAPTER 5

The Doctor

"Have you've heard what the Defense Advanced Research Projects Agency did with nanobots?" Sheila Arvarian, a neuro-ophthalmologist asked her dinner companions at the annual medical engineering conference.

"Yes, the implications are profound," answered a colleague. "They've gotten microscopic electrodes to move independently inside living systems."

"I think DARPA is trying to overcome the cerebral programming implanted in enemy soldiers by circumventing the neuronal chemistry with nanobots they would implant in their brains," Dr. Arvarian continued.

While some doctors applied political pressure on the country's leaders to reestablish peace, most continued practicing their trade without political involvement. Under the new unified civilian-military medical insurance system, everyone living within the Shield was served without regard for ability to pay. The new system permitted civilians and military personnel to see any doctor they wished. It regulated the fees doctors could charge, permitting few loopholes.

Doctors intent on getting rich went to work for the military, the only place where a practitioner could earn the kind of living medical professionals had become accustomed to. Because few outstanding physicians remained outside the jurisdiction of the Defense Shield, the drive for independent achievement was curtailed. Many groundbreaking research projects did not receive funding unless the military wanted them to. Alas, the price one paid for the security and relative affluence of connection to the military was to do the military's bidding.

As the war dragged on, the backlash commenced. Many promising medical innovations went undeveloped because young scientists decided not to devote their talent to military causes. Growing discontent among bright university students began to show itself in a drop-off in enlistments. Then there were the older and more established doctors, engineers, and scientists who, remembering the freedom they had before the war began, decided to go underground.

"How does cerebral programming work?" asked an engineer at the table.

A psychiatrist answered, "They use drugs to prepare the soldier's mind for programming, and then they undertake a long regimen of information injection. Through standard brainwashing techniques, they weaken the soldiers by isolation and malnutrition and break them down with fear tactics. Then they use cerebral programming—a combination of artificial intelligence implantation and neurotransmitter therapies. Then they build them up the way they want them to turn out."

The psychiatrist continued, "The effect is striking. Soldiers emerge capable of withstanding ungodly amounts of pain or, if necessary, ready to commit suicide. If captured, they can even program them to deliver misinformation in the face of torture."

"Practical military benefit aside," Dr. Arvarian pressed, "think about the technologies that our military would have to have at its disposal to counteract that level of mind control—cerebral programming, brain chemistry, control of brain neurology in unheard-of ways, information transmission inside neuronal systems with unprecedented agility."

"Why should the military be the only ones with access to this information? I think we could do great things with that technology,"

Dr. Arvarian persisted. She was doing her best not to be overheard, and her voice was barely audible. However, she had the attention of everyone at the table.

Sheila Arvarian would have commanded the attention of everyone at the table even if she were not making provocative statements. She was not only strikingly beautiful; she carried herself as one might expect for someone who had risen to the rank of full colonel in only ten years in the military medical corps. Dr. Arvarian had focused her career on applied research, believing that knowledge was worth nothing unless it was transformed into techniques and technology that made a difference in the larger scheme of things.

"You sound like you have something in mind," one of her colleagues said. "What are you proposing?"

"For one thing," she said, "I think we can give sight to the blind. Wouldn't that be a coup?"

"Yes, it would," remarked a specialist in visual cognition. "There aren't as many blind people around since genetic screening was made mandatory, but there are enough to make this a worthy project. Now that screening is optional. We'll be seeing more people with disabilities in the future."

"This is the first innovative concept I've heard in quite some time," the engineer opined. "I'm interested in hearing more. Just exactly what are you thinking?"

Dr. Arvarian was an outspoken advocate of open technology transfer. She had made a big splash developing methods to restore the damaged optic nerves of soldiers who suffered head wounds in battle. Still she hated the whole business of assisting the war machine and longed for peaceful uses of her skills. "Anyone who wishes to pursue the discussion is invited to join me for an after-dinner drink."

Since retiring to the bar would have been unwise as the conversation might have been overheard, Dr. Arvarian suggested they meet at a private room to hash out the details. After all, a group of eminent physicians and scientists discussing nonmilitary uses of technology ran against the grain. In fact, their conversation would have been construed as "contrary to the interests of the security of the homeland," so it was important that the room they chose was checked for microphones and imaging equipment, and that the conversation also include military applications such as helping permanently blinded soldiers to adjust to civilian life.

When they were safely behind closed doors, and the room inspected, Dr. Arvarian announced, "My concept is called the Intracranial Vision Device or IVD." She briefly outlined the project.

Optical receptor technology—fancy cameras that could duplicate the function of the eye—could take light energy and focus it toward the brain. Reconstructive surgery repaired many types of eye damage, even the retina could be replaced with artificial light receptors and transducers. The problem lay in what to do when the optic nerve and brain were not prepared to accept the input.

The group thought they could solve the puzzle. Microelectrodes, nanobots, could see to the task of assuring transmission of nerve signals from the retina to the appropriate brain centers. They could be employed to station themselves in places of healthy tissue and transfer signals through places in the brain that were damaged. Finally, cerebral programming would "train" the brain to efficiently process visual images.

"We can test people whose brains have never received visual input," she continued. "There are organizations we can call that can put us in touch with a pool of quality blind people. Some of them might be just dissatisfied enough with being unable to see that they will be willing to take a chance on our ideas."

"One thing that has daunted us since the beginning of time," a philosopher explained, "is the notion that visual experience is necessary for people to make sense of and quickly use the information brought to them by the eyes. Newborns begin to accumulate this experience almost from within the womb, reacting to light."

"The cerebral programming being used to prepare enemy soldiers contains the technique we need to encode visual experience," an expert in artificial intelligence offered.

"Are you suggesting that cerebral programming can replace the experience we accrue from the time we are born?" asked a psychologist.

"Yes," Dr. Arvarian replied. "We can chemically encode the visual experience of several adults, average these experiences, and provide a kind of 'template' upon which our blind volunteers will begin to build a new sensory world for themselves. In a short time, their own experience will blend with those provided by the visual-experience programming. Newly accumulated experiences will flow directly into the programming, and the programming in turn will become one with their experiences. Their sense of hearing will provide a cross-sensory framework. I predict they will integrate quickly."

Led by Dr. Arvarian, the group found money and shelter for the IVD provided by philanthropists who, disillusioned with curtailment of their ability to engage in venture capitalism, jumped at the chance to put their money into a nonmilitary endeavor.

"There's only one problem we haven't solved," Dr. Arvarian told them. "We need to find as yet un-invented technology to create the mobile electrodes that might be needed to help transport signals around damaged or undeveloped areas of the brain."

"What is the problem?" asked her engineer.

"If the technology isn't done right," she said, "these microscopic rovers could either fail to function at all or, worst case scenario, do a lot of damage."

She continued, "However, there is good news on that front. I know a brilliant doctoral student at the university who I think is almost ready to solve this problem."

CHAPTER 6

Deliverance

Diana looked up at the minister from just beneath the makeshift podium behind which he stood. To her inquiring mind, he seemed to be blurring the facts. Yes, she could agree, as Peter tried to tell the ancients, sometimes good things can come from destruction. Like the sulfur that destroyed the sinful cities or the rains that flooded the world, a missile had plummeted from out of nowhere to wreck the church, one of the few bulwarks of goodness, and hope her community still retained.

The military was still investigating. The initial consensus about how the missile penetrated the overhead shielding was a weakness due to power failure. Apparently the enemy had spotted it a while ago.

She called up to the minister, "We're not that bad, are we? We didn't deserve this, did we?"

"We are not bad people," he reassured. "Have faith that good will come from this terrible day. Follow your hearts, my children," he continued. "Love your neighbor as yourself and forgive your trespassers."

The minister stood in front of his congregation and looked out at a sea of faces earnestly seeking solace. Many stood while others sat in folding chairs or on the ground. Raising his eyes, he stared past the rear of the crowd toward the ruins of his church. A glint of metal, a still unremoved piece of *Satan's armor*, he thought, caught his glance. Overhead, wispy cumulous clouds floated; their cotton whiteness tainted slightly by the remnants of black smoke that had risen from the spot where his church once stood. Of necessity, today's services had been removed to a nearby ball field.

The crowd dispersed. The young woman made her way to the minister's side. "Is it possible for something to be both destructive and, in the process, portend salvation?"

"You are a very wise young lady," the minister answered. "What is your name?"

"Diana," she answered. "I am a scientist working for the very cause that may have led to the destruction of our church."

"What do you mean?"

"I can't discuss it, Father," she whispered. "I am a microbiotic engineer, and I don't know exactly to what end my work will lead. Suffice it to say, it's part of the defense initiative."

"Ah, then you have an appropriate name," he chuckled.

"Please be serious," she retorted. "I am not a huntress."

"But you are," he persisted. "You seek knowledge, and you will not desist until you have tamed your prey. Tell me," he prodded, "is your prey dangerous?"

"It is difficult to tell," she answered. "Besides, Father, I wouldn't tell you even if I knew."

"Then remember this," he admonished. "We must continue to love our enemies." Sensing his charge was not consoled by these words, he probed further. "What is worrying you, my dear? Do you believe that what you are doing might lead to more evil?"

"I'm not sure. Perhaps not," she shrugged. "It's just that one never knows to what good or what evil any scientific discovery might be used."

"If you have the foresight and wisdom, my young friend, to ask these questions, I believe your heart will lead you down the right path." He began to leave. Then he turned toward her. Looking her in the eye, he said, "Let that guide you."

The next morning, Diana returned to her lab. *The paramecium has nothing on you, my little friends,* she mused. Peering through an electron microscope, Diana watched her newest creations flit about in formations that would rival the best the Blue Angels had to offer. They swam within a salty fluid, turning in unison as they approached the edge of the container in which they resided. *You are the smallest and finest example of information technology, biotechnology, and nanotechnology ever assembled,* she thought. *I wonder if this is what it feels like to be a mother.* She brightened. *One thing is for sure, Dr. Arvarian will be so pleased.*

The young scientist had spent the last three years working to complete her doctorate. She was fortunate to be chosen as part of an elite team to work on highly secretive advanced military research. The goal of the project was to develop tiny robots that could roam the human brain and spinal cord.

"Why does the military want to do this?" Diana asked. As a graduate student and new member of the team, she was just naive enough to be surprised that asking such questions often resulted in stern rebukes. Still looking for an idea for her final doctoral project three years ago, she believed any opportunity to learn was an opportunity to be inquisitive.

"Let's just say, Dr. Arvarian, the team leader answered, 'We believe there has been developed out their brain technology that enables such vigorous programming of neural circuits that normal brain chemistry has been superseded. People thus altered cannot be restored through known biochemical methods. Our mobile nanobot technology will, hopefully, overcome this problem by shepherding brain signals around or even through damaged brain areas."

This explanation far from satisfying the young scientist. "What did she mean?" she asked her colleagues after the briefing concluded.

"Don't ask," they replied. "Obviously if Dr. Arvarian wanted you to know more, she would have told you. Besides, this level of discovery will no doubt have spin-off benefits that will win us a Nobel someday."

Now that a few years had passed, and the fruits of her labor swam in front of her, Diana swelled with the pride of a new parent readying her chicks to leave the nest. Speaking to her nanobots, she said, "The cilia work perfectly. You can move in any direction your programming dictates and with the agility of any one-celled organism nature has ever created."

The nanobots looked like a cross between a computer chip and a sleek single-celled organism. Three sets of protrusions spoiled their almost perfect octagonal shape. The larger cilia, hairlike structures barely visible at nano-level magnification, swayed to and fro and up and down, pushing the creatures in any direction in three-dimensional space the scientists desired. Other even more microscopic filaments could inject neurotransmitter chemicals into the synaptic space between neurons. These squirts could commence a process that resulted in anything from alteration of thought patterns to the creation of movement in a person whose brain or spinal cord might have been damaged.

Diana marveled. "The nanobots can talk to each other," she told her colleague. "I think I'll name them."

"Very funny," he replied. "How do they communicate?"

"They send laser signals to each other," Diana explained. "Lasers are wonderful. Their color and intensity can be adjusted to pass through subcellular matter without interference and without causing damage. We can send wireless signals all over the brain.

"The signals can be picked up by another nanobot's antennae. If necessary, they can relay information to each other, much like communications satellites do in orbit above the earth."

Dr. Arvarian entered the room and joined the conversation. "Most elegant of all, the nanobots can swim under the complete control of their programming, which also allows them to react to unforeseen obstacles and even to each other's presence."

Later at the press conference, Dr. Arvarian announced, "This is a major advance in brain and spinal cord research. Within the foreseeable future, we can hope to eliminate everything from schizophrenia to paralysis."

Diana went home that night feeling much better about her legacy. "At least on the surface," she told herself as she threw some leftovers into the microwave, "it appears my little darlings have lots of good work ahead of them." Yet when she peeked at her reflection in the door of the microwave, Diana could see the furrows in her brow growing deeper. She grew perplexed. "If I'm so sure about what I'm doing, then why am I still worried?"

Something in the science nagged at her. Could it be the energy required by the nanobots? Would difficulty in sustained power utilization be their Achilles heel?

As it happened, the energy cells embedded in the nanobots could store only sufficient energy for them to function for fifteen minutes or so. After that, they needed to recharge. They would replenish their energy by drawing on a variety of electrolytes present in the extra cellular environment. However, the process took time. If they were to be able to work continuously, the nanobots would have to work in "shifts." Given enough nanobots, this would be possible. Unfortunately because inadequate funding levels prevented the production of a sufficient number of them, the nanobots would have to be used judiciously.

I wonder what would happen if the nanobots learned to work in tandem? Could it be a 'force-multiplier' that might run amuck? The thought caused Diana to shudder.

She knew that from its inception, nanobot technology had been slated for use by the military and not necessarily always for humanitarian purposes. She recalled the complaints of the intelligence community about their inability to crack the secrets of captured spies and soldiers. Their brainwashing, it had become widely known, was thorough and effective. "We need a way to get inside the brains and minds of these 'sources.' Their brains are so hardwired," experts testified, "they cannot be talked down from their murderous mentality. When captured and interrogated, their minds are so well disciplined, no secrets can be wrested from them, save those their commanders want them to reveal."

As powerful as it was, the military's grip was not complete. A growing group of researchers had begun speaking out. They believed it unethical to limit the research to the narrow interests of the Defense Shield. Microsurgical techniques could be revolutionized, they insisted, if the same skilled robots could be programmed to venture deep within the spaces of heretofore impossible to reach places such as the core of brain or heart tissue. Some psychiatrists hoped the new technology could cure mental illness. Neuropsychologists had their sights set on the end of everything from Alzheimer's disease to learning disabilities. The existence of these conditions they insisted belied the contention that genetic engineering had eliminated all human "defects."

Others had even more specialized interests and desired to see just how far the nanobots could go. Chief among them were physiologists hoping to create perceptual advancements. Once again, technologies like advanced visual scopes and auditory sensors had taken the attention away from improving the human condition. The improvements being ignored included everything from the ability of soldiers to use their own eyes to see in foggy or pitch-black conditions or submariners learning to "hear" discreet sounds underwater. And of course, only a few scientists like Dr. Arvarian thought that this type of basic research could not only improve the sensory functioning of soldiers and sailors but might possibly bring hearing to the deaf and sight to the blind.

CHAPTER 7

The Search

Eventually I met Dr. Arvarian. She told me about the project that had brought us together. The "vision creation" team perfected their procedures by experimenting on dogs and various primates. When they were certain their scheme would work, they contacted blind organizations and asked for volunteers.

Much to their surprise, the organized blind movement didn't jump on board. Embracing the "cure" was not at the top of their list. The scientists assumed they would be overrun with willing participants, but the blind community was reticent. For one thing, it feared drawing the ire of the military community, which still held the power to replenish at least a portion of the funding for beneficial programs that had been removed over the years.

"What makes you think anyone would wish to risk their lives on your procedure?" the president of the blind organization asked. "Do you have government sanction for this project?"

Dr. Arvarian, representing the team, was prepared for these questions. She had been coached in the various philosophies of how blind people regard themselves and how they wanted society to treat them. "Our project is privately funded. We have followed proper research procedures. Our work has not been published in the mainstream scientific journals because doing so would be premature. In fact, before we continue, I must ask you to agree you will not officially publish information about our research. We have come to you because we know about your philosophy toward government intervention and your distress at the removal of government support for innovations and social programs that would make life better for people who are blind."

"I am still dubious," the leader replied. "Besides, most of our members have worked out ways to be happy and fulfilled while being blind. You may get volunteers, but I suspect they will not be sufficiently adjusted to be trustworthy."

"We have developed a rigorous screening process," the doctor replied. "But due to limited funding and technical resources, we can only provide people with the ability to see for short periods of time. They will remain blind when the device is inactive."

"Interesting," the leader mused. "Because the technology can provide vision for limited periods of time, it means that the artificial vision could be used simply to offset the most inconveniencing aspect of blindness but not negate the necessity for people who are blind to learn appropriate skills of blindness to live full and happy lives."

"That is right," the doctor answered.

The leader, partially won over, said, "I will only commit my organization to providing your contact information to those who call us specifically asking about such a possibility. We will neither endorse nor condemn the project."

Dr. Arvarian breathed a sigh of relief. This was the break she had sought. "We accept your offer." *Once people learn about our project*, she thought, *we will surely find a sufficient number of qualified candidates.*

The applications began to flow in. Mine was the first through the screening process.

CHAPTER 8

Dan

Dan was born into an army family. His dad was a chef. His mother was a force field specialist, a physicist who helped develop the massive power source required to generate and maintain the protective electromagnetic shield that eventually surrounded the country. "Because of your mom," Dan's father would say, "no intruder can penetrate the national border by air, land, or sea. Because of me, no soldier need ever worry about going hungry! Neither will you."

Dan thought, *My father feeds me well, but he's never gotten used to the fact that his only son was born blind. Sometimes I hate him for making me feel so small.* He chuckled at his next thought, *And sometimes I hate him for making me feel so large.*

Indeed, Dan had grown stereotypically fat and jolly, helping his father in the mess hall, eating more than his share of army grub. He carried more girth at an early age than was healthy, but also carried a quick sense of humor about things. "I may be blind," he'd call out playfully to the soldiers on the chow line, "but I can always find my way to the food!"

To his credit, his father saw to it that Dan developed a strong work ethic. "If I have to make you an assistant cook," he would say, "you will grow up to be a working man. No sitting around."

Dan's mother, a scientist of a far different temperament than her husband and who worked for the military because that is where the jobs were, provided Dan with his ability to take an easy-going stance and shrug things off. This skill held him in good stead whenever his father became overly domineering. "Don't worry," she said whenever she saw Dan's face tense with anxiety, "you will find your own way in this world."

Dan's parents couldn't figure out why their son had been born blind. They had both passed many physical examinations over the years. Since there was no history of "genetic imperfections" in their families and since both of Dan's parents were military people, suggesting a natural genetic predisposition to any child of theirs becoming a soldier, only first-level screenings were undertaken during his mother's pregnancy. Obviously they'd missed something.

Dan was an anomaly. Because of this, his parents pampered him. Growing up in an army family meant he got to live in several parts of the country. To his detriment, he had little chance to form lasting friendships. Playing alone much of the time, Dan was forced to fight his own sociable nature, becoming self-absorbed and reclusive. This was outside his comfort zone, but because he was not athletic, and his extra pounds engendered lots of teasing from schoolmates, he protected himself by shying away from them, even when he wanted to join them.

"Come on, fat boy," a school bully taunted. "See if you can hit me."

"All right." Dan laughed, thinking he would try to lighten the situation. "Bring it on"

Unfortunately the tormentor sneaked up on Dan and, without warning, punched him and grabbed his lunchbox. "Come take your lunch back," the bully chided.

Dan lunged at the boy, missing him by several feet and falling to the ground. The bully laughed and tossed the box toward where Dan lay sprawled in the dirt.

"Leave him alone," a teacher shouted.

The bully scampered away.

The teacher retrieved the box and handed it to Dan, who managed to get up. Dusting himself off he said, "Thank you." Then hugging his lunchbox and with tears rolling down his cheeks, Dan said, "I'm sure he didn't mean any harm." Then he found a table and ate lunch alone.

In the end, if it were not for the fact that he was noticeably different, Dan's classmates would probably not have missed him on those numerous occasions when he failed to show up for school in September. His "disappearances" occurred every two or three years when one of his parents was transferred. Either his father would be ordered to another perimeter site or his mother would receive a new project. In any case, Dan often found himself either minus one of his two parents for several months or packing up and moving during the summer to a new town or city.

Left alone with no one to play with, Dan amused himself with fast food and rock music. Often secluded in his room, Dan soon developed an active fantasy life. He read science fiction, dreaming of a day when people would be virtually bionic. Any part of them that didn't work well would be replaced. Artificial body parts could take someone like him who couldn't fight their way out of an old-fashioned phone booth and convert him into a Superman.

Someday, he said to himself, *I'll have lots of friends and won't worry about beating the crap out of anyone who teases me.* Putting aside thoughts of violence, he imagined what life might be like if only he were not blind.

Dan lay back in his bed, head resting upon large pillows fluffed and made ready for him by his mother. As his thoughts strayed toward fantasies of being the most popular boy in the class, he fell asleep and dreamed.

The autumn shadows covered the edges of the field. The sun blocked by the bleachers, jutting high over the players diving and tumbling in the thick grass. Short-skirted teenage girls leaped and cartwheeled on the sidelines. It was Saturday, and the score was tied. Dan was the quarterback, the boy for whom the girls cheered most loudly. He stood under center awaiting the snap.

"Go get 'em, Danny," the coach yelled.

"Hike!" Dan shouted. The football struck his hands as the center's body, lunging forward, melted away from his touch. He heard the thud of shoulder pads as his trusted linemen crashed into the defensive guards and tackles whose bloodcurdling yells he knew were meant for him. Gripping the ball with his right hand, Dan straightened and backpedaled.

Dan knew the play by heart. The image of where each receiver would be in a few seconds and where his blockers were fixed firmly in his mind. He believed he was in total control of not only his own ten teammates but all eleven players on the other side of the ball.

Dan heard the sound of a 250-pound linebacker thundering in his direction. Hell-bent on destroying him, the massive defender had penetrated the line and was now contriving to penetrate Dan's chest.

"Ball!" Dan heard his favorite receiver yell from far in front of him. Instantly and with power beyond expectation, Dan snapped his right arm forward. The ball spiraled down range, arching toward the center of the goalpost. The receiver ran underneath the ball; the linebacker smashed into Dan.

In the stands and on the sidelines, the crowd roared, "Touchdown!" As usual, he was able to pick out from among the few thousand people the voice of his favorite girl. It seemed, no matter how far he moved from her on the gridiron, Dan always knew where to find his girlfriend in the stands. Smiling, Dan looked forward to receiving lots of affection from her after the game. Later that evening, as she cuddled into his arms, he would quip, "This sure beats football!"

Awakening, Dan opened his eyes. Although he sensed the world similarly in his dreams as when awake, somehow the world seemed less bleak inside his dreams than outside them. With the implausibility of his fantasy weighing upon him, Dan shook himself free of his reverie. Allowing himself to regress, Dan buried his face in the pillows, which comforted him as his mother's bosom must have so long ago, and cried. Gulping, he murmured, "I'll never be that guy on the field." After a few minutes of determining to end his self-indulgence, he lifted his head and said, "Somehow I'll find a way to be happy in the real world."

A flicker of strength filled him. "Dreams may be for fools, but I'm not going to give up." He resolved, *I guess it's up to me to make my own way in life.*

With the fantasy of success on the gridiron galvanizing him, he let his thoughts drift to a seminal question. *I wonder what it would be like if I could see?*

In fact, Dan became obsessed with the question. He tried to learn everything he could about what it is like to see. He asked his most trusted acquaintance to describe his eyesight. Driven to the point of annoyance, the friend relented and tried to answer.

"It's hard to put into words," he said. "Light enters my eyes, and my brain creates moving pictures. I don't know how. I just see. That's all."

"It must be exhilarating to have all that information and light flooding into your head," Dan speculated.

"I guess it is wonderful," his friend said quizzically, "but it is normal for me. It is all I have ever known."

"How do you see a football as it's flying through the air?"

"That's hard to explain. I have to keep my eyes on the area in the sky where I think the ball might be. Then I see it and try not to take my eyes off of it after that."

"I don't think I'll ever understand how you can see things." The concepts were simply too arcane for Dan to imagine.

"Try this," his friend attempted. "When you hear a moving vehicle, can't you track its location with your ears?"

"Sure," Dan replied. "But I don't have to keep my ears pointed toward the object."

"Oh, you sort of do," his friend responded. "If you don't turn your head at just the right moment," he pursued, "you will lose track of the object's exact location. Your hearing is similar in many ways to my vision. You're trained to use your ears, and I'm trained to use my eyes. That's all."

In an uncanny rush of intuition for a teenager, Dan's friend searched for a silver lining. "Vision isn't so special." His friend soothed. "You're doing just fine without being able to see. We all like you. Besides," he added, "there's a lot in this world I wish I couldn't see."

"What do you mean?" Dan asked. *Why would anyone wish to have no eyesight?* he thought.

"There's a lot of responsibility that comes with seeing," his friend explained. "I have no excuse for not being aware of things around me."

"Neither do I," Dan retorted. "Do you think I am not aware of the things I can't see?"

His friend was puzzled by Dan's reaction. Why wouldn't Dan take the "break" nature gave him and let some of the bad things in the world just drift on by? Backtracking, he said, "I guess your hearing tells you an awful lot," the friend admitted. "But believe me," he went on, "there are lots of ugly things in the world that I wish I had never seen."

"Such as?" Dan challenged, bristling at the notion that anyone would try to convince him that not seeing was somehow better than seeing.

"I've seen dead animals on the roadside, bull of blood, and all smashed up. I've seen bodies without limbs on the news. They carry them out of wrecked buildings and vehicles after earthquakes and bombings. It's terrible. You should be glad you've never seen some of these things."

Figuring his friend took the good things his vision gave him for granted because he had always had access to them, Dan decided to press on. "If I could see, I'd be popular in school. I'd be an athlete. The girls would pay attention to me. I go out for football. I'd drive a great car, and nothing would get in my way."

"That's a bunch of bull," his friend retorted. "You're not a bruiser. You'd make a lousy football player. If you could see, you'd probably still spend most of your time reading, eating, and hacking away on your computer."

This gave Dan pause. He had to consider whether his friend might be right. Perhaps even if he were able to see, would his true nature be different? "What is my true nature," he asked himself. "Is what I do the same as what I am? If it is, then I am a hermit by nature."

Dan struggled with this riddle for a long time. A week or so later, he brought up the topic with his friend again. "I'd definitely drive a nice car," he stated confidently, "and have lots of friends, go to dances, and have a girlfriend." His image of himself as an extravert would be realized someday. In the meantime and with additional thought, he decided, "Perhaps it might be better if I take a different tack. Instead of dreaming about joining the football team and fretting over things I can't do right now, I'll concentrate on getting into a good college. I'll get there somehow," he promised himself. "Wherever that may be."

After graduation, Dan enrolled in a computer systems course at the local community college. I met him during new student orientation. One of my jobs as an intern career counselor was to help incoming students choose a course of study.

Dan was fascinated with me. "I've never met another blind person," he said. "It's amazing. You are actually working for the college."

"In a manner of speaking," I answered, "I am interning here. I attend the university."

"Have you ever been able to see?" Dan inquired.

"No, why do you ask?"

"Lately," Dan admitted, "I've been obsessed with wanting to know how people see. Have you ever wondered what it might be like to see?"

"Yes," I said. "Life has many frustrations that would be a lot easier to deal with if we had eyesight. What do you think?"

"I think you are absolutely right. I've wanted to be everything from popular in school to a football player. Now," his voice trailed off, "all I'm trying to figure out is what to do with my life."

"That's what we're here for," I stated. "What have you thought about doing?"

"If I can't become a star athlete or learn to operate a military vehicle, I'll create something useful to the world. I really am much more a lover than a fighter." He chuckled.

When Dan started college, the economy was at a particularly low ebb. In an effort to consolidate resources, students from the nearby arts college took their computer classes at Dan's community college. In turn, students from Dan's school trooped to the arts college for many social activities. This turned out to be fortuitous. The arrangement facilitated Dan's meeting a girl.

One Friday evening, Dan found himself at a dance. Overwhelmed by the noise and too shy to wander about the dance floor without an escort, he cowered as far from the din as he could. Sitting in a chair along the edge of the dance floor, he muttered, "This is ironic. Here I am, guarding the perimeter, and without weapons, I've retreated."

While Dan sat, waiting for something to happen, well-meaning friends noticed the situation and surreptitiously matched him up with a blind woman they saw standing near the edge of the dance floor. She seemed to be having trouble connecting to dance partners. They led her to him, and before Dan knew that she existed, he felt her body land in his lap.

CHAPTER 9

Carla

The news that their newborn daughter would never be able to see affected Carla's parents badly. "How could this have happened?" Carla's father complained to the doctor. "We were screened, and no one told us that our daughter might be born blind."

"We were so much counting on sharing our lives and our work with her," Carla's mother added between sobs. "She'll never be able to appreciate the things that we find so joyful."

The pediatricians said they didn't detect the gene that caused Carla to be premature. They managed to delay the delivery as long as they could, and when she was born, they immediately placed Carla into a dark and oxygen-rich environment. Despite full awareness of what might happen and even though they used the best vaso-suppressant medication, the doctors were unable to prevent her blood vessels from proliferating and essentially destroying Carla's retinas.

"Is anything else wrong with her?" her mother pleaded. "If one part of her was damaged, weren't other parts also damaged?"

"We don't see signs of anything else having been affected," the doctor answered. "We'll just have to let time go by and keep an eye on her. If anything else has happened," he concluded, "it will be subtle."

As Carla's parents took their new daughter home, their sadness was especially compounded, for they were painters devoted to the visual side of sensuality. In fact, Carla's mother was known for her voluptuous nudes. Her father was famous for his portraits of notorious men in history; their images depicted in surrealistic watercolor.

Learning that Carla would not be able to see crushed the hope their daughter would appreciate this aspect of their world. They even wondered if Carla would ever be able to appreciate any aspect of the sensual. After all, they concluded, weren't even the smells of flowers made richer by their bright colors?

Carla's parents joined a Buddhist community in California. The community taught them that to cope, they must find the good in everything. They were taught that Carla's way of apprehending the universe, although different from their own, could—if given a chance to flourish—be as fulfilling as theirs.

"How will she ever appreciate the things we see when we look at the world around us?" her mother asked. "Will she ever have the feelings that come with a sudden rush of beauty that can only enter the soul through the eyes?"

"They say," Carla's father added, "the eyes are the window to the soul. How can her soul be enriched if her eyes don't work?"

The teacher answered, "All that seems to be is not truth. Very little in the universe is set in stone. Things change. We evolve. So will you. Your happiness and that of your daughter is not doomed to failure. There is more than one way to the soul. The eyes need not be the only way to profound truth and beauty. If you choose to believe in a soul, you will find that the richness of the world comes to us in many ways and takes many forms. You must let it flow to your daughter."

Wanting to believe, Carla's parents accepted their teacher's words. They resolved they would fill their daughter with as much sensuality as they could through her other senses.

"I trust our teacher's perspective," Carla's mother said. "But how can he be sure?"

Her father answered, "They told us that knowledge comes from many sources. I guess we'll have to have faith that somehow Carla will absorb the glory of the world. Perhaps we are so fixated on vision we can't accept that there may be other ways."

"I hope you're right," her mother answered. "I'll certainly do what I can to make sure our daughter experiences the fullness of life."

Determined not to view the world through their disappointment, Carla's parents decided to show Carla the things they loved through her sense of touch and verbally describe as much as they could. They hoped that this would imbue in Carla the same regard for the sensual that they so dearly enjoyed. Carla's mother would take the lead in executing this strategy.

As soon as Carla was old enough, her mother began taking her to museums. Through touching the statues, Carla learned the immense pleasure of the human form. Her mother arranged these explorations during off-hours so no one would think them prurient. Carla felt embarrassed and, at a primal level, frightened when touching the statues, especially the male figures. After a while, she began to protest.

"Mom," Carla complained one day as they drove home. "I'm getting tired of going to the museum. I feel strange touching those statues. Isn't there something else we can do?"

Carla was nearly thirteen years old. While her mother was doing her best to expand her daughter's artistic and sensual awareness, she didn't seem to be aware that she might be prematurely arousing Carla's sexuality. Even at such a young age, Carla realized that it wasn't healthy to feel the combination of emotions she experienced. The juxtaposition of arousal and fear began to do psychological damage. Although not quite able to explain it, Carla knew enough to beg her mother to change her approach.

Her mother got the message. She diversified their forays. She included female and animal figures and didn't press Carla to explore the males. Unfortunately an undefined craving had planted itself within her. Unconsciously she tried to sublimate her feelings by overindulging at the dinner table. She snacked frequently between meals. Worse, behind her parents' back, she began to binge and then, worried about gaining weight, to purge.

Meanwhile, Carla's parents applauded themselves for how well their daughter had developed an affinity for the sensual. However, she was overprotected. Her parents were not teaching her much about the pragmatics of life.

For example, although they saw to it she learned to read Braille, Carla was nearly a teenager before her parents permitted her to learn to travel outside her neighborhood and school alone. "She seems to lose her way quite easily," they complained to Carla's teacher.

"Yes," the teacher observed, "I've seen her get turned around in the classroom and fail to find her way out the door and down the hall."

The mobility specialist said, "This is more common with kids losing their sight when born prematurely than the literature has been able to empirically show."

"What can we do?" her father asked.

"Practice and lots of repetition," the instructor answered. "We'll have to teach Carla to maintain her attention span so she will not lose her orientation. If she is as attentive to her senses as you say she is, she will use the feel of the sun when outside and all of the sounds and touches around her, and things will work out."

As Carla grew into her teen years and became more aware of her body, comparing it with the angelic female figures she had touched in the museums, she realized that she would have to be careful with what she ate. The binging and purging thankfully had stopped on their own. Unfortunately images of cavorting and well-endowed masculine figures occasionally insinuated themselves into her imagination. This forced at too early an age an intensification of her sex drive. Lying in bed at night, she struggled with feelings she did not know how to handle.

Carla didn't want to give up food, so to have her cake and eat it too, so to speak, she asked her mother to help her exercise more. This helped but wasn't emotionally satisfying. So she read a lot. She grew especially fond of romantic novels. With heightened senses, an isolated and self-indulgent environment in which to grow up, and plenty of opportunity to use her imagination, Carla began to confuse the difference between romance and indulgence. By the time she reached puberty, she had both a longing for and a fear of intimacy.

Carla grew good at manipulating others. In high school, she had become an expert at getting boys to escort her everywhere, help her with her schoolwork and, most of all, provide her with much-needed companionship. Her hook was the implicit message that she would give them something in return for their protection.

When they obliged her request to walk her to class or take her to dances, she allowed them to take just enough liberty with her, that eventually some of them took more advantage of her than she wanted. As inevitably as contact with a flame is followed by pain, the thought stabbed into Carla's consciousness. "I'm disgusting," she told herself. "They treat me like what I am, a slut."

Around this time, Carla was beginning to come to another realization. Her inability to appreciate the visual arts may have been more painful for her parents than they realized. *I can't give them the thing they want most,* she sadly admitted to herself. *I'll never share the rush they get from looking at a painting. Nor will they ever be satisfied with my level of appreciation of their world, so long as they believe that seeing it is the only way.*

In her struggle to please her parents, Carla had never considered doing anything else with her life except art. She may have had the potential to be lots of things, but by limiting her horizons, Carla would never know it. "I am once again taking the easy way out," she said to herself. "After all, why bother to figure out what I am interested in doing if the world is not my oyster." Limiting her search to an artistic vocation was Carla's way of ending her parents' disappointment.

Luckily, Carla found music. She not only liked it, she had talent. She could play and compose. Piano became her mainstay. And she could sing. One evening, her hands traversing the ivories, she mused wryly, *All the finger work on those statues finally paid off.*

Because her grades were a bit too low, the local arts college admitted Carla on the basis of a successful audition and her parents' reputation in the community. In high school, except for her music courses, she had barely managed to pass her other classes. "I hope you realize," the admissions officer told her, "you are going to have to produce good and independent work in all your courses, not just music, and right from the start."

"In high school, I always got help," admitted Carla. "I guess it's time I start doing things for myself."

"Exactly. The first thing I want you to promise is that you will take a room in the dormitory and learn to get along without your parents."

She did, catching up admirably in her freshman year, and not just in her studies. She joined a workout and weight-control class. She learned how to use a computer and began to compose. She even picked up a piano gig at the campus coffee shop.

Carla's repertoire included everything from moody love songs to raucous sea chanteys. This increased her popularity with the boys but not her sense of well-being.

Her roommate provided insight. "You're doing it again," she said. "I don't mean this literally," she proceeded, "but in effect, you're selling sex to the boys. The only difference is that this time, they are paying to see you instead of you paying them for their attention."

Carla thought about this and agreed. "You've really sunk to a new low," she quietly admitted to herself.

She decided the best thing to do was to protect herself from her own impulses. Instead of relying on others, Carla studied hard and refused all requests for dates. Not only did she do well at the coffee shop, she earned high grades in her college courses. To reduce temptation, she even allowed her mother to convince her to come home every weekend. "We can eat healthy food instead of that dormitory stuff and take in a museum once in a while."

One weekend, Carla decided to remain on campus. For some reason, her roommate had been urging her to attend an upcoming dance. "Why are you pushing this dance?" Carla asked. Her roommate had been talking about the music, the boys, and the illicitly procured alcohol for days. "You are driving me crazy."

"Everyone will be there," her roommate answered. "Besides," she continued, "Don't you want to meet someone? It's a great place for having fun. You don't have to do anything but dance if that's what you're worried about."

As expected, the dance was too loud and crowded for Carla's taste. Her roommate, also as expected, had disappeared into the crowd, leaving Carla to her own devices. Carla tried to listen for male conversation, thinking she might walk straight up to a group of boys and ask one of them to dance. Then she remembered that in the past, the sight of her cane seemed to be enough to cause most boys to grow nervous and seek an escape. She decided to use a trick someone had taught her and slowly walk the perimeter of the room with the hope someone would say hello to her.

After a while and when her tactic wasn't working, Carla began to feel lonely amidst the crowd. She truly wished she hadn't let her roommate talk her into coming. Growing tired of the din and the isolation she felt within it, she plotted a strategy to extricate herself. Carla moved as far from the surround sound as she could. Then she began looking for the exit.

Observing Carla's maneuvers from across the room, her roommate ran up to her. "Why aren't you dancing?"

"I can't hear a thing, and no one has come up and asked me," Carla complained.

Speaking directly into Carla's ear, she announced, "There's a great looking guy sitting over there. His name is Dan, and he's also blind. I'll get you in front of him, and then you're on your own." Before she could protest, Carla found herself being pushed, first to the left and then backward.

A very surprised yet deeply resonant voice penetrated the music. "Excuse me. Sitting on my lap may be an interesting way to introduce yourself, but it's no way to treat a fellow you've never met."

Carla clambered to her feet. Turning to face him, Carla said, "I'm so sorry." Her voice automatically taking on the seductive tone she had mastered in high school. Then remembering the consequences of that behavior, she stepped back and tried again.

"I'm sorry. My name is Carla."

"I'm Dan. That certainly was some greeting!"

"It was an accident. I can't see. Don't read anything into it," Carla retorted.

Experience had taught her to beware of men once they'd made physical contact. Usually, that was the signal for them to go further.

Fortunately for Carla, Dan was an easy-going guy. He could have been brazened and quipped about how nice it felt when Carla landed in his lap. He could have gotten defensive and said, "Hey, you sat on me. I didn't do anything wrong." Instead, he decided to be gentle.

Shouting above the din, Dan pursued. He said, "I know you from the coffee shop. You play a great piano. You sing well too."

"Thanks," Carla answered. "I enjoy it."

Guessing that Carla wasn't any more comfortable trying to have a conversation in the midst of so much noise than he, Dan took a deep breath and suggested, "How about us going to the coffee shop? At least there, we'll be able to hear each other. I'll buy you a cup of coffee." Then he chuckled. "I promise. You won't have to play for me."

Sitting in the relative quiet and familiarity of the coffee shop, Dan's easy-going demeanor allowed her to become engulfed in their conversation. Carla began to relax. Grateful to escape the dance, she was glad she had agreed to Dan's suggestion. Nothing seemed to bother him, not even being blind. Forgetting to worry about what would happen next, Carla realized she was enjoying herself.

When it was time for the evening to end, Carla was again pleasantly surprised. Dan escorted her to the dorm and didn't attempt to get into her room. Instead, he simply said good night and gently squeezed Carla's hand.

Then he surprised her again. Instead of leaning in for a kiss and the perfunctory bit of body contact that women expect men to attempt, Dan moved toward the door and announced, "I'll see you at the coffee shop."

"Okay," Carla answered, wondering why the evening wasn't going to end like so many others had. Surprised by the lack of lecherous intent, Carla was ready to feel insulted. *He isn't pursuing me,* she thought. *Maybe he doesn't find me attractive. Or perhaps he's gay.*

When Dan left not having attempted, well, anything, Carla thought, *Strange behavior for a man. It doesn't seem he wants more from me than friendship. Well*—she chuckled—*perhaps he's waiting until the second date.*

Carla understood more than she realized. *Despite his gregariousness, perhaps Dan was shy*, she thought. He had told her enough about himself for her to comprehend he carried the self-image of a person burdened with two disadvantages. With both a disability and a weight problem, Dan preferred to make friends first and ask questions later. As she listened to Dan walk away, cane tapping as he did so, Carla smiled. She thought, *Maybe my life of debauchery is about to change for the better.*

Settling into bed that night and with a warm glow to keep her company, Carla realized that for the first time in memory, she felt clean at the conclusion of a date. Then as if dredged up from the primal ooze, a wave of nausea coursed through her body. "Who am I kidding?" she muttered. "I'm dreaming. This can't be real."

Carla lay still until the feeling faded. Confused about whether to trust Dan or any man and exhausted from the evening's emotional roller coaster, Carla finally allowed herself to be overtaken by sleep. Then she really dreamed.

The garden smelled fresh. Clear water flowed over rocks from an unknown source above, splashing in a brook at Carla's feet. She bent forward and swept her hand through the cold water. Around her stood several dozen stone statues lined up like so many soldiers, each depicting famous men. Many were nude, muscular, and well-endowed. Poses ranged from that of the pugilist poised for delivery of a knockout punch to gracefully smooth dancers stretching their limbs to the extreme.

Carla could feel their presence. Some emanated heat; others were just warm. None moved. However, one felt cold to the touch.

Carla shivered as she walked past it and moved away from the apparition as quickly as possible. Unable to put the feeling into words, it was clear to her that this hunk of carved rock bore her ill will

It stood with legs poised to spring; knees slightly bent. One foot was forward of the other. Its head bore lines that marred an otherwise smooth face, like so many scratches from fingernails of yore. The eyes were half shut; the mouth fixed in a grimace. The statue seemed to Carla to have her in his sights.

The brook grew quiet. In the relative silence, Carla heard something moving toward her. She didn't have to see it, for in her dream, she could not, but Carla understood that the man was coming for her. She backed away, turned, and tried to run. She ran several steps only to find her path blocked by the wall that surrounded the garden.

Cold sweat collected on Carla's forehead and neck. She felt her spine tingle. The petrified menace was close now. Carla instinctively folded her arms around herself, attempting to squelch an uncontrollable wave of fear.

Cold hard hands clamped around Carla's arms. "You sent for me?" a harsh voice asked.

Carla tried to speak, but nothing escaped her tightened throat. Her lips felt parched. Despite her fear, she could think only about drinking from the gurgling brook. *This is absurd*, she thought. Then she thought again, *What is he going to do to me?*

The hands moved to Carla's neck. "You sent for me?" the voice asked again.

No, I didn't, Carla thought. Her voice still failing her. *Leave me alone.*

The hands grasped her collar. Carla tried to pull them away. Instead, she felt her arms, heavy and immovable, pinned to her side.

Then Carla remembered that all she wore was a nightgown. She was truly vulnerable.

The hands pulled Carla to the ground, and the stone body lay upon her. Carla began to suffocate under the immense weight. She felt his member press against her and realized his intent.

Carla freed her hands, reached for his face, and jammed her fingernails into the man's eyes. *I'll make you just like me*, she thought; words still failing to pass her lips.

The man roared with the pain Carla imparted but continued to press against her. As Carla felt the stoneman tense with the pain of her scratching him, she felt a perverted pleasure in having done some damage.

Carla felt hot breath upon her ear. Enveloped by the confusion of fear, pain, and libidinal stimulation, she finally managed to scream. The man's face contorted. Then Carla awoke.

She sat up, thankfully safe in her bed. Carla began to cry. "Who will protect me?" Sad her parents couldn't hear her, Carla realized just how alone she was. "I wonder. Can anyone protect me?"

CHAPTER 10

Dan and Carla

Carla tried to put the nightmare into perspective. She told her roommate who woke up when Carla screamed about the dream. "It's the remnants of things from my past," she summarized. "My mind is trying to tell me not to drop my guard, not even for a nice guy like Dan."

"But Carla," her roommate pleaded. "Not every man is a rapacious maniac. Look," she suggested, crawling into bed with Carla and hugging her, "talk to Dan. He might have some ideas."

A few days later, they sat in the coffee house, having lunch. "You should get a guide dog," Dan encouraged. "You're a beautiful woman, and you would be even more beautiful standing on your own two feet, moving swiftly instead of slowly like you do with your cane. You don't need to lean on me or any other man."

"No one has ever encouraged me to be on my own." Carla sobbed. Her tears came as much from Dan's generosity as from the realization that if she didn't take care of herself, probably no one would. *A guide dog would, indeed, help me be more independent,* Carla thought. *Also, it would provide me with protection.*

"It took meeting another blind person to open my eyes to the possibilities," she said to Dan. "Okay, I'll do it." Hugging him, she said, "Thank you."

ꟹ

Something else was bothering Carla. "As much as I would love to sleep with him," she told her roommate, "I can't bring myself to do it."

"Why not?" her roommate chided. "Are you suddenly a prude?"

"No," Carla answered. Continuing, she complained, "I know what it is. So many blind people don't get enough exercise." She went on hesitantly, "I'm ashamed to admit it, but I'm turned off by his weight."

"That's okay," her roommate comforted. "Just tell him you will be more amorous if he takes off a few pounds. He'll want you so much, he'll start dropping inches before you know it.

"Are you sure you aren't afraid to make love? That dream might have meant more than you think. Do you suppose you might be using Dan's weight as a convenient excuse to keep your distance?"

"I hadn't thought of that," Carla answered. "I think I'll tell Dan how I feel about his weight. If he loses weight, and I still don't want to sleep with him, I guess I'll know."

ꟹ

To Carla's surprise, Dan relented easily. "Okay, If you are willing to get a guide dog, I'm willing to lose weight."

Carla felt guilt about the demands she had made of Dan. Sad memories of cruel rejection surged to the forefront of her thoughts. She recalled being dumped by her date after her senior prom. Grateful for a wonderful evening, Carla believed she had owed the boy his pleasures. Unfortunately, after having his way with her in the back seat of his car, he told her goodbye. "You're not my type," he said cruelly. Then he dropped her at her front door, leaving Carla sobbing and sick to her stomach to stagger into the house. There her parents, after ascertaining what had just happened to their daughter, tended to the job of helping her pick up the pieces.

In retrospect, Carla realized just how harmful the entire experience had been. "Better to be alone with your self-respect than with someone who hurts you," she concluded. Now she had to decide whether to trust Dan enough to give their relationship a chance. Imagining Dan had his own stories to tell about loneliness and rejection, Carla decided she would take the risk.

Carla graduated college with a degree in music. Dan completed his computer systems degree. She went to guide dog school; he joined an exercise and weight-loss program. She became a concert pianist. He became a shield systems programmer.

Carla landed a job with the city orchestra. Her parents were proud, for landing such a coveted job right out of college was rare. Carla was good, the maestro conjectured, because of her feel for the sensuality of the music.

Dan was hired by a military contractor and immediately consulted with his mother for a shield designer's wish list. This gave him an advantage over most programmers who rarely had a feel for the concerns of their end users. Thus, he was able to hit the ground running, contributing to his design team almost from the first day on the job.

In the romance department, love trumped lust. Dan and Carla's affection for each other made "waiting" easy. It did not hurt their relationship. In fact, their growth as people coincided with and drove their desire for new and more adventurous ways of enjoying the pleasures of each other. Eventually Dan and Carla began to wonder what it would be like if they could see each other's faces. "I'll bet it would be a rush," Dan speculated.

"Yes, it would be a rush," Carla answered. Taking it a step further and thinking about the pleasure her mother seemed to derive from looking at paintings and statues of male nudes, she added, "I'd love to know whether seeing your body is the same as touching it."

At that moment, Carla realized she had a deeper longing. Voicing her feelings more strongly than she'd intended, she amplified, "I also want something else. I want to be able to see paintings and sculpture so I can talk to my parents about their art. Without direct experience, all I've been able to do is pretend to know what turns them on."

"You really feel strongly about this, don't you?" Dan replied.

"My parents are brilliant painters, and I've never been able to share their joy. Wouldn't it be neat if I could be a real part of that aspect of their lives instead of only the daughter they had to take care of all these years?"

The next day, they sent applications to Dr. Arvarian.

CHAPTER 11

The Screening

Dr. Arvarian welcomed me to her office. After I was seated, she asked, "Why do you want artificially induced intermittent vision?"

I sat alone with her in what I imagined to be a sparsely decorated office. Although I couldn't see it, the room seemed to be devoid of the usual trappings of a doctor's office.

"I can't say for sure, doctor," I yammered. "All I know is that for the most part, I can get through the day quite well without sight. But there are those moments when I know that if I could only see for a few minutes or even ten seconds at a time, my life would be much easier."

"What do you mean?" she queried.

"A few weeks ago, I took a promotional examination that was full of charts and graphs that I could not decipher. The person assigned to assist me to take the exam would not explain them. Of course, I did poorly on that portion of the exam and did not get the promotion. If I'd had vision, even for a few minutes, I would have been able to do much better."

"That certainly seems to be an event we might call life-altering, but is it a good reason to risk major brain surgery?"

"You don't understand, doc," I pleaded. "There are so many things that people take for granted that are not at all trivial when you don't have them. Try finding your way to a building that you've never seen before. It could be ten or a hundred feet away, and you might not know it. The security guards stop and question you, and then they still let you flounder. A person you might ask directions of could be a hand wave away, but you wouldn't know they are there. Or as is usually the case with everyone trying to get off the streets as fast as they can these days, there's no one around to help you.

"Surely there are devices that can help with locating things in the environment," Dr. Arvarian posited.

"There were several in various phases of testing a decade ago," I answered, "including devices that interface with the Global Positioning System, and even devices that could send images to powerful recognition computers or even to a friend, and they could tell you what is in front of you."

"What happened to them?" the doctor asked.

"They were defunded," I replied with a sour tone. "And here we sit, floundering over the smallest things that are still the big things for us."

"Worst of all," I continued, "because she wants to be complimented, I pretend to know how pretty my girlfriend, Cheryl, looks. It hurts me because obviously I'm aware that she's quietly accepted I really don't know what she looks like for sure."

"Those are strong motives," the doctor agreed. "But I have to remind you that you would still have no eyesight most of the day. Having the use of your eyes even for fifteen minutes out of twenty-four hours might make you want to see all the time," she pursued. "Could you live with the fact we are unable to give you that?"

"Yes, doc," I assured her. "I'm pretty much okay. I just need a little help once in a while. I would not have blown that promotional exam had I gotten the right kind of help, but I am convinced that I would have done better with much less muss and fuss if I could just have looked at the charts and graphs for even a few minutes."

"Besides," I continued, "I don't see why it's unreasonable to expect I wouldn't want to use technology that could take me as far as the IVD can."

Like a good number of blind people, I had grown particularly disappointed over the years at missing out on the benefit that technology could bring to us if only it weren't being withheld by the government. Since it discontinued putting money into several special public works programs, such niceties as talking electronic signs, an efficient public transport system, and several projects designed to provide the public with universal information access were lost to us. These were only three of many things that would have made day-to-day life easier.

Dr. Arvarian persisted, "The IVD has not been totally perfected. I must be sure you realize that."

I wasn't sure if the doctor was serious or dissembling. Was this part of the screening process to test my motives and resolve? I decided to take the bait and plunge in. "Why hasn't it been perfected? Are we part of an experiment?"

"The technology we've used to design the IVD is adapted from several sources. Some of it is still classified by the Defense Shield. You and three others will be the first to receive the IVD," Dr. Arvarian answered.

"So I've got to be willing to take a chance on the technology going wrong and another chance on getting caught by Homeland Security?"

"Yes to the first question," the doctor answered, "and no to the second. No one will ever know you have the technology inside you unless you tell them. We will require you to maintain total secrecy until we know that you and the rest of your group have fared well with it."

"Who else knows about this experiment?"

"It's not as much of an experiment as I may have made it sound," Dr. Arvarian said, trying to alleviate my angst. "To answer your question," she went on, "a research team of engineers, physiologists, and psychologists, to name a few, contributed to developing the Intracranial Vision Device. I assure you there are a lot of people out there who care about helping rather than hurting."

"Who else has been accepted?"

"You are our first candidate," she answered. "We will let you know who the others are after they have been screened into the program."

She continued, "Installing the IVD will require extensive surgery to place the robotic electrodes in your brain and the neuro optical retinal implants in your eyes." Then she frightened me. "We also are not totally sure how you will react to mobile electrodes traveling from place to place in your brain."

Growing alarmed with an image of swarming insects roaming and feasting inside my head, I choked out, "Why will the electrodes be able to move around in my brain anyway?"

The doctor reminded me that mobile robotic implants would simplify the surgery by reducing the number of fixed electrodes the medical team would have to plant in there. The possibility of unwanted side effects, such as infection or unintentional destruction of brain tissue, would be minimized. The electrodes would send signals from the eye to the visual centers of the brain, including the occipital lobe where visual memories are stored, and awareness of vision is made possible. She continued, "Now here is an important question. Have you ever been able to see?"

"No," I replied, knowing this fact, plus good health, were basic acceptance criteria for the procedure.

She responded with a reassuring tone, "We'll test you to be certain. We need to make sure you weren't born with vision that is now long-forgotten."

"Why is that important?" I asked.

The doctor explained, "We can't chance your having visual experience that might interfere with the programming we will provide you. The electrodes will then 'get used to' the impulses that will be coming from your brain, including those from the visual memory in the programming I just mentioned."

Dr. Arvarian chose not to highlight the fact that the research had not been approved by the government, and that the project was the result of many scientists pursuing their dream of enhancing the human capacity, including providing sight to the blind. They had risked their careers to overcome decades of limited government support for nonmilitary projects.

Vision is a complex matter. However, the team thought its approach and design were elegant. First, the eyeball was examined to make sure it possessed all the structures necessary to conduct light to the optic nerve. If it didn't, they substituted artificial lenses and corneas. They even inserted photoelectric implants to take the place of the retina. If the optic nerve turned out to be damaged in a particular patient, multichannel neurofibers were substituted. Used in conjunction with electrodes attached to the retina, they sent signals to robots waiting at the midbrain. Signals would be transmitted to the visual cortex and other parts of the brain, including those concerned with movement, hearing, and language, to name only a few.

"Remembering and relating what you are seeing to things you know about and translating this understanding into action all require instantaneous response," the doctor explained to me. "Thus, to facilitate these activities, we have elected to use as much of the body's existing neuronal structure as possible and to coordinate them with the electrodes."

As for me, I didn't care as much about the mechanics as being able to occasionally see what was going on around me. The doctor said that it wasn't quite that simple. Just because my eyes might work again, she admonished, I might not be able to make sense of the enormous amount of input my brain would be receiving. That is why an extensive amount of cognitive programming was part of the protocol.

"Your brain has nothing visual with which to relate," she informed me. "Your eyes will be able to see, but without several terabytes of visual experience implanted into your head, you won't be able to make sense of anything the eye sends to your brain. In fact, without some way to understand exactly what you are seeing, you won't be able to keep from getting overwhelmed by all that input. In all likelihood rather than use your vision, you will either avoid turning on the IVD or simply close your eyes when you do."

The examination continued. My head was jammed into a helmet. The doctor fired light impulses through my dormant eyes into the photonically virginal interior of my cerebrum. When no reaction was forthcoming save that which was ordinarily expected of a live brain hit with millions of units of electromagnetic energy, I was pronounced fit for surgery.

"Well, you are the first of your group to be screened," the doctor said. Then lowering her voice as if a coconspirator, she continued, "You will be considered the leader of your group. We screened you first because we consider you the most thoughtful of the four top candidates. We will expect you to give good counsel to the others and to keep us informed if anything unexpected happens to any of you."

"When will I meet the others?"

"After the screenings are completed and the surgeries take place. In fact, our plan is for the four of you to become a team. We expect you will provide each other with a great deal of support."

There was a knock at the door. Dr. Arvarian pressed an intercom switch and asked who was there.

"It's Diana," the voice came back.

"Great! Come in, I have someone I'd like you to meet."

Thrusting a small but firm hand into mine, Diana said, "I'm pleased to meet you." A vibration surged through my body. While I didn't know that she was an important part of the science team, I did know that she was having a definite sensual effect upon me.

"Same here," I answered, trying to maintain an air of clinical distance. Hoping she didn't see my temples throbbing, I asked, "How do you know Dr. Arvarian?"

Drawing up a chair, she replied, "I helped develop the nanobots."

"So you're the one responsible for the little bugs that will be running around in my head." By now, Diana's perfume had wafted toward me, and I wanted to know as much about her as a woman as a scientist.

Dr. Arvarian, sensing my various "interests" in Diana, thought she should intervene. "Diana is responsible for making sure that the electrodes do their job well. She is part of the postsurgical follow-up team. She will be keeping a close eye on you and your group."

"That's reassuring," I replied with genuine gratitude. "I'm glad you scientists also have a heart."

"Of course, we do!" Diana answered. The emotion in her voice betrayed seemingly strong feelings about it. "We won't let anything happen to you."

"Well, if there are no further questions," Dr. Arvarian interjected, "we should call it a day."

Shaking hands with the doctor and, lingeringly, Diana, I left the office and went home to tell Cheryl that something big was about to transpire.

The next day, Joe came in for screening. He entered the room, quickly oriented himself, and immediately impressed the doctor with his ability to think spatially. "You will be the most athletic of the group," she told him. "Moreover, you will probably challenge the IVD in ways the others won't dare to do."

"How do you know?" Joe asked. "Did your psychological profile tell you that?"

"In fact, yes, you will probably use the device in ways we haven't thought of. We will be in close contact with you through routine checkups, so if you begin to overdo it, we will let you know."

Dan and Carla passed their screenings in similar fashion.

"We hope, Dan," the doctor said. "You will maintain your fitness program and use the IVD to challenge your brain's ability to absorb geometric figures and mathematical formulas. Your daily work should provide plenty of opportunity for this."

"Carla," the doctor said. "We think you will be a most interesting user of the IVD. Your love of the sensuous, things that cause the emotions to rise, will tell us just how well the IVD interacts with the rest of the body."

"We plan to use our bodies a lot," they quipped in unison.

"Good for you," the doctor encouraged. "The surgeries will take place tomorrow. Are you ready?"

I was ready, but Cheryl was not. Always reliable for her levelheadedness—in this case, she seemed anything but. Since we had met in college, she had coaxed me through moments of doubt and uncertainty. Now it was my turn to help her.

"I'm afraid you're going to die," she blurted. "Why can't we just go on the way we've been?"

"I know this conversation isn't going to be easy," I attempted to soothe.

"Please listen to me," she cried. "You are putting yourself at tremendous risk. Are you that unhappy with your life the way it is?"

"No, sweetheart," I answered. "It's just that the inconveniences are starting to mount up. That promotional exam was the straw that broke the camel's back. It's a matter of survival. If our society was more supportive," I continued, "I wouldn't dream of doing something like this."

"Besides," I added, taking her hand, "don't you want me to see how beautiful you are?"

"I don't care if you know how I look," she screamed. "Are you so shallow as to think I care about that? Or is it that you think I'm that shallow?"

"I'm sorry, Cheryl," I stammered. "I just thought you'd want me to be able to compliment you."

"And what?" she snapped. "Do you think I need it?"

"Well, yes, I think." It was dawning on me that I'd stepped into something much more complicated than I'd realized. In the past, we'd had a few disappointing discussions about what it was like for Cheryl knowing that her boyfriend couldn't actually see what she looked like. Other men could see her, and Cheryl had confessed that it made her feel good knowing that they found her attractive.

This usually ended the conversation. Jealous and angered by my helplessness around this issue, I generally changed the subject. I had even stormed away on occasion, telling Cheryl I knew full well what she looked like, and that it wasn't fair for her to dwell upon the subject.

"Don't you remember telling me about all those guys who give you the eye?" I asked.

"Oh my god," Cheryl groaned. "Did you take that to mean I wanted you to be able to see me? That's not what I meant. I was just bragging a little and letting you know what a great guy you are to me."

Realizing that I had truly misunderstood and feeling bad, I drew Cheryl into my arms. I pressed her face into my shoulder, and she began to cry. "I only wanted you to know that you were dating an attractive woman. I figured that if you knew other guys looked at me, you would feel assured you weren't going out with a dog. It was my insecurity," she added. "Not my need for you to see me."

I hugged her tightly and assured her that she need never have worried about how I felt about her. "Now I can't wait to see you," I said. "Who would want to miss out on all that?"

"You're so full of it," she rebounded. Then choking back tears, she concluded, "You're going to go through with it, aren't you?"

"Yes," I answered, "not because of any one thing but because of everything. Please," I begged, "stay with me and wish me luck."

CHAPTER 12

The Gang of Four

The surgeries, the doctors told us afterward, went without incident.

A few days later, after recovering from the ordeal of having tiny microchannels drilled through our skulls, and optical wafers inserted to replace our retinas, the doctors brought the first IVD group together for introductions.

Everyone was surprised that Dan and Joe knew me. "It's a small world," I reminded the members of the follow-up team who had assembled with us. "There aren't that many blind people out there to begin with."

Joe and I were introduced to Carla who immediately sized us up. "I'll bet you will be the philosopher," she said to me. To Joe, she quipped, "You're going to be the macho one in this group. I can tell."

Joe retorted, "It's a good thing I'm a man of old-fashioned values, and that you're Dan's girl. Otherwise, I'd show you my macho."

I held my breath, expecting either Dan or Carla to chastise Joe for being too forward. To my relief, I heard them laugh.

Later, after listening to my flirtatious banter with Diana who had joined us in mid-meeting, Carla added, "I see you never met a beautiful woman you didn't like."

Embarrassed, Diana answered, "Don't worry, I'll make sure he doesn't get any more attention from me than the rest of you."

"That's good," Joe quipped. "I want a chance to learn all about microbiotic engineering too!"

"So long as that is all the engineering you intend," Diana dinged, "we'll be just fine."

Joe slumped in his chair in mock resignation. Everyone chuckled.

"That's great, folks," Dr. Arvarian said. "You've just had your first of what we are sure will be many encounters. As a group, I believe you had just successfully gotten through your first honest attempt at communication." Later the doctors and I agreed. Members of the group would not have any trouble telling each other how we felt.

Next, as the doctors had outlined, to hasten the adjustment of our brains and minds to optical input, we underwent vision programming. The short training program taught us about light and dark, points and lines, movement and nonmovement, simple and complex pattern recognition, and on and on. Most important, we were trained how to integrate the sights we would soon be seeing into our everyday rhythms. The goal was to maintain psychological stability amidst the deluge of new and powerful inputs we would receive.

The doctors were right. The first time I saw anything, I was shocked by a flood of sensations. I felt both overwhelming fear and abundant energy course through my body. My head was wrenched with pain as light flooded into what had been a relatively dark and quiet place. I closed my eyes to restore peace.

After a while, my tolerance increased, and I became motivated to keep my eyes open. Things I saw began to make sense to me on a more consistent basis.

The doctors told us to walk across the testing room. This led to immediate fatigue. It felt as though our arms and legs were made of jelly. Joe assumed the role of coach. "Come on," he urged. "This is just like learning to skate."

"That's easy for you to say," Dan chirped. "You're a natural athlete. I'm a newcomer to physical fitness and still a klutz."

"Hang in there," I encouraged.

"That's right," Carla chimed in. "We'll just have to put one foot in front of another until we get normal again."

Dr. Arvarian and Diana applauded. "That's the spirit group. Just listen to each other, and you will be fine."

After a while, our confidence grew stronger. We even began to feel our body strength increase. Although we knew this was probably an illusion, the result of an adrenalin surge, it sure felt exhilarating. A few weeks of hologram and other cognitive therapies followed, and we were ready to resume our lives.

The doctors set up a schedule of follow-up visits with each of us and another schedule for the "gang of four," as I called us to meet with each other for mutual support.

"We will be monitoring you in a few different ways," Dr. Arvarian, our chief contact from now on, instructed. "We will ask you to stand every night in front of a scanner we will place in your homes and allow the nanobots to send us daily telemetry. Diana will monitor both you and the nanobots."

"That's right," she offered. "The nanobots have all been given names of a sort. I can tell the condition of each of them by a special signal we programmed into them."

"Can you control them from the distance?" Carla asked.

"No," Diana and Dr. Arvarian answered in unison.

"Why do you want to know?" asked the doctor.

"I wouldn't want my mind being tapped, or my privacy invaded," Carla answered pointedly.

"Don't worry." Dr. Arvarian laughed. "We will only be able to tell if the electrodes are working and how hard."

"Yeah," Joe jumped in. "So, Carla, if you and Dan get too rambunctious, they'll know!"

"We won't be able to tap your brains and see what you see," the doctor reassured.

"Or what you are doing," she glanced at Diana.

"One other request," Diana announced. "The scanner is small enough, so if you plan a trip, please take it with you."

"Yes," Joe said, throwing a gentle punch into my shoulder. He said, "Your scanner will spend more time at Cheryl's than in your own home!"

I laughed. "Don't worry, Joe, your turn will come." Then I thought, *Well, there goes my chance to make time with Diana.*

"Also," the doctor continued, "we will ask you to meet with each other once a week to discuss your experiences." Referring to me, she said, "Your team leader is responsible for knowing how you are doing and for making sure problems get solved. Please keep in touch with each other and let your team leader know if anything unusual happens."

"Do we have to report every time we make love?" Carla joked.

"Yes," I said. "Every time and with details."

"Dream on, bud," Dan chimed in.

"All right, gang," the doctor reasserted. "Unless we see a need for more frequent visits for the next year the designated trial period to which you have agreed, you will need to come into the office for checkups only once every three months. We've been monitoring you, and you are all doing splendidly. We are very happy."

The doctor had a final caveat, "There is only one other requirement. You have signed papers, but we want to remind you that under no circumstances, must you tell anyone about the IVDs."

"How will that work?" asked Joe. "If we use the device at work or anywhere among people who know us, won't they realize something is different?"

"Yes," the doctor acknowledged. "You will tell them you've had surgery and have had some of your vision restored. Tell them it is not reliable, and your eyes get tired after only a few minutes. They will not know that your newfound eyesight comes from the IVD. They will think it comes from more conventional surgery."

"That works for me," Dan agreed.

"Me too," added Carla.

Happy that the group seemed to be in accord, the doctor sent us on our way. We left the hospital, knowing we were essentially no different than before the procedure except that we had a new and powerful tool, if not on our hands than in our heads!

Somehow though, despite the reassurances of Diana and the doctor, we felt just a little anxious. Nevertheless, despite their exhortation toward cautiousness, we also felt invincible.

Diana gritted her teeth and stared at Dr. Arvarian. Pretending not to notice, the doctor jotted notes in her log. Finally, she asked, "What's the matter?"

"Why did you lie to them?"

"To which lie are you referring?"

"Oh my god!" Diana groaned. "What else have you omitted from their briefing?"

"It's for their own sanity that they believe they have their privacy," the doctor declared. "As for anything else you believe about your little progeny, you should trust that the development group knows what it's doing."

"I trust that there will always be a difference between right and wrong," Diana expostulated. "Please promise you will remember that, doctor."

Diana picked up her briefcase and coat and prepared to leave.

"I hope you will remember that we have made history. We've taken technology meant for war and done something good with it."

"If you confine your activities to what you promised me," Diana replied. "I will be satisfied if we are staying within ethical bounds. The last thing I need is to be another Oppenheimer."

"My, my." Dr. Arvarian laughed. "We certainly are full of ourselves, aren't we?"

Diana looked at her; fear and uncertainty etched on her face.

CHAPTER 13

The Days

For the first time in my life, I thought I was truly happy. Was I dreaming? Am I dreaming now?

I traversed the days as much as I always had, leading the life I'd always led. I went to work, cavorted with my girlfriend, worked out at the gym, and conducted my life as I'd done before.

Most of the time, I continued to do things the old-fashioned way. The few technologies I owned, and whose evolution had been thwarted by the war machine were still there, but when the going got tough, I dared to use the Intracranial Vision Device.

I pressed a button mounted on my wrist, and radio pulses activated the optic receivers which were implanted into my eyes. The nanobots picked up the signals, and the world instantly and vividly flashed into view.

Initially, I was quite cautious in using the IVD. My first solo effort took place in my bedroom. I wanted to see, well, anything. Then I tried looking at myself in a mirror. That didn't work well as making sense of a reflection was harder than I thought it would be.

Next, I used it to make sure the new clothes I had just purchased looked good. That, too, was more difficult than I had anticipated. First, I struggled to recognize the colors and put names to them. Then I struggled to remember what I had been taught about which color combinations actually constituted a match.

I consulted my neighbor to confirm that I had made a correct choice. "Yes," he said, "the tie is brown with stripes, and your shirt is light tan. A good match. Don't forget to match the pants as well."

"No problem," I said. "I've got my clothes labeled and pre-matched. I just wanted to know if they looked good to you."

Emboldened, I next activated the IVD to locate the front gate of my apartment complex from a distance. Enhanced security measures since the days of the initial terrorist attacks included high walls, which surrounded and protected all residential and business cooperatives. They had a characteristic pattern, bulletproof and bombproof facades, imbued in environmentally appropriate colors, and broken only where entrances had been constructed. These entrances, gates positioned far apart and protected with crash barriers and foliage that made them hard to find, had always been difficult for me to locate. They were so well disguised that when visiting a new place, until making physical contact with them, I wasn't always sure where an entrance might be.

The IVD made it easy. Activating the system and taking a quick look, I could now joyfully beeline straight for the desired portal. No more dragging myself along walls like a burglar sneaking up on his prey. No more having to convince wary guards that I was not a terrorist.

The thought of what it would be like when I saw Cheryl's face for the first time was most anxiety-provoking. How would I know if what I was looking at was beautiful or ugly? Since I'd already made myself believe she was beautiful (my ego would accept no less), what would I do if I found her less attractive? How would I even know? The only thing I had to go by, I figured, were the emotions that I might feel when I saw her. How would I act if I was disappointed? Would I hurt her feelings?

"Just call her on the videophone," Joe said during one of our group sessions. "You can activate the IVD and see her image from the safety of your own home. Then," he continued, "if you have a bad reaction, you can always find an excuse to get off the phone."

Dan wasn't sure. "I've got a bad feeling about this," he warned.

"You are a coward!" Carla interjected. "And, Joe, you are terrible for suggesting it," she admonished. "Just face her and do it," Carla went on. "I'm sure you won't be disappointed.

Then in as stern a voice as she could muster, Carla ordered, "Just in case, remember this—don't you dare show Cheryl any disappointment. Just live with it. Tell her you love her. Don't be a pig."

I felt awash with guilt. My face flushed with embarrassment. My plan had, indeed, included a surreptitious call to Cheryl on my talking computer phone and engaging the video display. I thought if I saw her for the first time from the safety and distance of a computer hookup, my reaction would be less obvious than in person. I didn't really think I would have a negative reaction to my girlfriend's appearance, given her delightful personality, my tactual explorations of her face, and all we'd been through together. Still, anticipation held me in its grip. Thanks to Carla, my sense of right and wrong was back in place.

Resolving not to use the IVD until I was face-to-face with her, I set up our date.

Turning on the computer, I activated the telephone connection software. "Telephone ready," the synthetic voice announced.

"Hi, honey," I greeted.

"Hi, sweetheart," she replied. Her innocent voice sent surges of pleasure and guilt through me. Cheryl trusted me, including my fidelity, something no matter how macho I might get on occasion, I had never betrayed. In fact, since my conversation with Cheryl the night before the surgery, I'd never been more in love with her.

"Sweetheart," I blurted. "How about dinner tonight?"

"It's a work night," she answered, somewhat perplexed. "What's the occasion?"

"I need to see you," I said with just enough coyness in my tone for her to get my drift.

"Sure," she answered. Then with a barely discernable tremor in her voice, she said, "I want to see you too."

I knew Cheryl was anxious waiting for the time I'd be ready to use the IVD to look at her. Although she never let on, I knew she was as nervous as I was about how I would react the first time I saw her.

"Remember what we said that night?" I asked. "You have nothing to worry about."

"I know," she answered softly. "We can call for takeout," she proposed. "Come on over."

It took me a half hour to shower and put on clean clothes and another half hour to walk to her apartment complex. In the meantime, Cheryl had ordered food and otherwise prepared for my arrival. Our rhythms and thoughts synchronized, we both knew this would be a night to remember.

By the time I arrived, the food had been delivered, and its aroma wafted from the warming oven. I smiled as I thought if it had been me, I wouldn't have known whether to plan for the food to be eaten right away or to be kept warm for a while. For that matter, what if we had a bad time, and the food never got eaten at all?

"Hi, beautiful," I greeted when Cheryl opened the door.

"You didn't turn it on already, did you?" she cried. "I wanted it to be special."

"No, I was just teasing." I laughed. "Besides, I don't need to see you to know you're beautiful. You know that."

The humor had served its purpose, easing the tension. Cheryl took my hand and led me to the middle of her living room. "Before we do this," she announced, "I want to give you something."

"What?" I asked.

Without a word, she pulled me toward her, planted a long kiss upon my lips, and pressed her body firmly against mine. It was not as much a sexual maneuver as a comforting and loving exchange of closeness—something I don't think I'd felt as completely before that evening.

Releasing her grip and stroking my face, she teased, "Go ahead and do it, big boy. Take a look at me."

I held her at arm's length in front of me and pressed the button on my wrist that wirelessly interfaced with the IVD. The nanobots commenced firing and roaming. In a split second, a wonder crystallized before me. I found myself staring into clearer blue eyes and sweeter lips than my fantasies could ever have imagined.

Feelings came in a rush. I felt surges of adrenalin and warmth all over. Twinges of activity throughout my body confirmed that something good was happening. "You are beautiful," I blurted.

"You're really looking at me!" she exclaimed. "I've been wondering what this moment would be like. It's a good thing I don't wear much makeup," she went on. "I'd be a mess right now."

Tears streamed from Cheryl's eyes, causing her face to glisten in the dim light of her living room.

I felt myself well up inside, and then I, too, began to cry. This moment had meant more to both of us than we had thought it would. I wondered, *If she's as beautiful as I thought she would be, was it worth putting ourselves through this torture just to find out what we already knew?*

Cheryl let me look at her face for what seemed to be hours. In reality, it was only five minutes—five luscious minutes. Then she let me look at the rest of her. An hour later, the IVD long since turned off, we sat at her table, our robes thrown on as an afterthought, languidly feeding each other wonton soup.

"What was it like for you knowing that I was really seeing you?" I asked as we cuddled on the couch.

"I almost hate to tell you," she answered slowly, "but it was a sexual rush. I think women are programmed not by nanobots but by society," she trailed off and began to sob again. "Why is it so important how others think we look?"

I thought, *For once, keep your mouth shut and just hug and kiss her*. And so I did.

The "gang of four" met regularly once a week for camaraderie and to share experiences. We talked about what we had used our IVDs for and what we thought and felt about what we saw. We talked about the practical applications for which we used our newfound vision, who wasted time on trivialities, and who was most virtuous. We even debated whether my experience looking at, say, an automobile moving toward me was the same as Joe's or whether Dan's experience of a painting could possibly rival Carla's. Hadn't Joe trained himself to conceptualize perspective better than me? Hadn't Carla been trained by her parents to appreciate the subtleties of art?

The novelty of our visual experiences and the reinforcement of discussing them with our fellow "visual virgins" (as Carla liked to call us) lasted for a while and then began to fizzle out. After the first time, for example, I didn't even bother to activate my IVD for the meetings. Why waste the minutes looking at folks I knew so well? We even began to critically examine the power of vision to give us true happiness.

I wondered aloud if we hadn't bowed to "visual prejudice." "We've been handed a bunch of bull," I opined one day quite out of the blue. "I've used my IVD in all sorts of situations and haven't found much to get off on."

"What do you mean?" Carla implored. "I think it's great to see the flowers and sunset. Haven't you gone to the movies yet and used your IVD during those quiet sexy scenes? We have."

"No, I haven't needed to. I can figure that stuff out for myself," Dan chimed in, "Come on, man, don't you enjoy looking at your girlfriend's face?"

"I did for the first few times, and then I memorized how she looks and don't use my minutes for that anymore," I offered." How about you?"

Dan said, "I get a rush every time I look at Carla. It's much more of a turn-on than just remembering what she looks like in my head."

"Have you compared your reactions to things, like art or a sunset?" Joe asked.

"In fact, we did look at some paintings together, but we really couldn't explain to each other our reactions beyond, 'Oh, that looks sexy,'" Carla chirped.

She continued; her voice sounding exasperated. "By the way. You men are impossible. Don't you know women need to be reassured that you love us on a regular basis? I'm certain Cheryl would love it if you looked at her every time you were together."

Joe chimed in, "This is trivial. I've got plans of my own and need way more than the fifteen minutes they've given us." Directing his next comment at me, he said, "I think you're off base. Being able to see is great. I want more. Enjoy it for all it's worth. Soon you'll be wanting more, too.

"Come on, Joe," I answered. "Aren't you happy with what you've got?"

"You aren't being adventurous enough. Don't you see what's happened? Blindness has taken the wind out of your sails. The difference between you and me," he pursued, "is that I've got a plan to get the wind back into mine"

Joe's comment confused me. While he was angry because he didn't have a sufficient number of "vision-minutes" in a day to pursue his dreams, I was arguing that vision wasn't all it had been cracked up to be. The others also had different views than me. Dan thought I was being a bore and told me to lighten up and enjoy life. Carla couldn't fathom how I would ignore the sensual potential in being able to see.

I clung to my argument. "Vision doesn't truly have the importance to our happiness that society places upon it. All you need is to adjust to your situation, and the things you don't have won't seem so bad."

Joe reminded me, "Weren't you the one who argued with the doctor when she didn't understand about the importance of having even a little vision?"

Joe's comment derailed my train of thought. The duality of my viewpoint struck home. To be content with one's situation or to strive for something more: Those were, indeed, the questions.

Why, after so much discontent and risk, was I backtracking? Why, seemingly out of nowhere, had I forgotten the myriad things I wasn't able to do because I couldn't see? Had I experienced a second epiphany, one that had somehow obliterated my vision dream? Were the snippets of vision I'd already absorbed sufficiently fulfilling to satiate my longings? Or had I simply gotten lazy? After all, possessing vision removed a potent rationale from my defenses. What excuse would I now have for, say, blowing a promotional exam?

Carla, on the other hand, used her newfound vision with gusto. The first thing she did after a few trial runs was to pay a visit to her parents. "Mom and Dad," She announced, "show me your paintings."

"What are you talking about?" my mother asked.

"I'll explain in a minute, Carla answered. "Just show me a painting or two."

When Carla reacted to the sight of the painting with an emotional display her parents had never seen, her mother gasped. "What did you do?" Ignoring doctor Arvarian's admonitions as had the rest of us, Carla explained the surgery. As they absorbed the information and began to understand the implications of what had occurred, her parents were both shocked and pleased. Carla's mother was especially happy. The initial trepidation that momentarily threatened to stop her heart was allayed by elation. Finally, she would be able to show her daughter the wonders of sensual art.

Her father was not as pleased. "How could you take such a risk without telling us?" he demanded. "Don't you know how dangerous this is?"

"I knew it would make you happy if I could see," Carla rejoined. "It's what you've always wanted. It's what I've always wanted too." She began to cry.

"Can these devices in your head hurt you?" her father asked. His voice had changed from strained to a more analytical tone. Carla thought she could hear the tentative beginnings of acceptance and forgiveness.

"The doctors are quite sure everything will be all right, so long as I don't overuse the device."

"Well," her father offered, "let's just take this one step at a time. Go look at more of your mother's paintings." Then as an afterthought, he quipped, "It's something you girls need to do without a man, throwing a wet blanket on your fun." Winking, he left them alone.

Carla's mother provided her with a feast of sensual art. Her eyes rested on male figures for long seconds at a time. She felt emotions surge in ways that touching statues, and even the real thing hadn't evoked. *Could the visual be this enticing?* she wondered. *Why should it be so powerful? After all, I've encountered these things tactually quite often.*

Carla quickly learned she didn't have enough minutes of vision to do more than closely examine a few paintings per session and still have some vision in reserve for her trip home. "I want to keep a minute or two in reserve in case I get into a jam while traveling out there," she told her mother.

As she walked home one day, a flicker of alarm kindled in Carla's mind. "This is addictive," she told herself. "I can't wait to examine mother's next painting." She thought, *I've experienced this before, this addiction, but not as rapid and powerful as now. Maybe I'm my mother's daughter more than I thought. Is this the bond my mother has been missing all these years?* Putting aside worries that she was having too much fun and succumbing to the lure, Carla decided not to spoil the artistic and sensual possibilities with silly stoic hesitations.

Her mother agreed. "Allow yourself to get into the art," she told her daughter. "Soon, it will become part of you. Then if you are willing to try, I'll teach you how to paint."

❧

Dan decided to return to college. "With my fifteen minutes a day," he predicted, "I'll be able to get a degree in aeronautical engineering and really get into high-tech design."

His workdays had become boring. Dan's coworkers knew he was anxious to add to the creative process during planning meetings and noticed his frustration when they began talking about designs he couldn't fully visualize. The conversations quickly overwhelmed him, and when he could no longer contribute, he typically sank back into silence and listened as the planning meeting droned on around him.

"I've got to be able to do more than take on the busy work the team hands me," he complained to us during one of our sessions. "What can I do to keep up when the team starts pointing to minute parts of the diagrams and making rapid design changes?"

"Is it really that hard?" Joe asked. "I can keep up with the schematics in the aircraft design work I do."

"Yes," Dan assured. "When the team gets on a roll, the diagram changes as soon as they key into the computer a new parameter or object. My tactile diagrams are outdated two seconds after they print one for me. There's no way I can keep up unless I can recreate the new image in my head."

"So much for the refreshable tactile graphics displays they were working on," Joe quipped. "The static ones work great, but they can't produce fresh new diagrams in real time, which is what you need."

"Why, Joe," Dan gushed, "you really understand this stuff."

"What do you think you could do?" I asked.

Dan thought for a long moment. He was so quiet, I was tempted to turn on my IVD to make sure he was all right. Suddenly he spoke. "That's it," he concluded, slamming his fist on the table. Rising to leave, he announced in a voice so loud it frightened Carla, "I'm going to do two things. I'm going back to school, and I'm going to use my fifteen minutes of vision per day to make a splash."

Dan had another problem, one he couldn't confide to the group. Lately, Carla hadn't been as "friendly" to him as in the past. Yes, she still seemed to like him, and yes, they still made love on weekends, but the nature of the lovemaking had changed. Carla seemed dissatisfied, performing the act quickly and almost wantonly. She didn't seem to want to savor the moments as in the past. Moreover, Dan found himself disappointed after they were done.

I can't figure it out, he thought. *We both reach orgasm, that's still true, but she doesn't linger. There's also no foreplay anymore. It's as if she isn't interested.* He decided to confront the issue.

That conversation left Dan even more worried. Carla confessed to Dan that she had become so absorbed in the overly idealized sensuality of her mother's paintings that her image of him had changed. "I'm sorry," she sobbed. "I just don't find you as sexy as I once did."

Then trying to help Dan salvage his ego, she went on, "It's not fair to you, and it's not your fault. No one can compete with the males in mother's paintings. I don't know how Dad has put up with it all these years."

Dan recoiled. "I feel like a fool," he told Carla. "While you've been getting into such great shape and developing a sex drive that I can't keep up with, I've just been going along thinking everything is fine. I've lost a lot of weight, but apparently that's not good enough."

"I don't want you to change yourself for me anymore than you already have," Carla declared. She reached to touch him only to find Dan so inconsolable that he pulled away from her.

"Don't worry," he said, "I won't do it for you. I will, however, do it for myself."

With that, Dan hired a personal trainer and began working out. His body tightened up, and for the first time in his life, he noticed muscles bulging in his arms. He went so far as to ask Carla to show him some of the paintings that had inspired her so he could get a sense of the idealized male figure. "Not that I can become like them," he said, after perusing a few paintings depicting well-endowed Adonises, "but I can always dream."

Dan even tried tennis. "This is putting the IVD to its ultimate test," Dan told the doctor during a routine checkup. "Tracking a small ball through the air is the most fantastic thing I could ever have dreamed."

"All the exercise will help your weight-loss program too," the doctor added. "You certainly are using the Intracranial Vision Device in a way we hadn't thought about. Have you tried throwing a football?"

Dan answered, "Yes, but I haven't found it nearly as interesting as my fantasies. I guess there's more to the thrill of sports than one simple act. Without a team and a crowd and all the practice that goes behind competition, the thrill just isn't there."

The doctor sympathized, "Keep up the good work and continue to uplink to our monitors at night so we can make sure you're still okay."

They hadn't told us initially, but after we had been out in the world for a while, the doctors began to worry that the plans to monitor our physiologies had been incomplete. Yes, the nanobots had capabilities that made it possible for them to individually send signals to the doctors' computers, but we humans still needed to sidle up to a telemetry device for the doctors to evaluate our status on a daily basis. In order to be more complete, they added monthly visits to the hospital for a more thorough checkup.

As it turned out, Joe needed closer scrutiny than the rest of us. He didn't know it, but he was suffering from several by-products of his origins.

One of the reasons cloning had been such a fearful phenomenon in its relatively short history was the travesty most people felt it made of the human condition. "It is an unnatural act to produce a human from methods that do not involve an egg from a female and a sperm from a male," went the dictum. There also were grave scientific concerns about what might happen to a cloned human as he grew older. "We have little experience to inform us of the likely complications if any that might accrue to a human clone as the aging process continues."

On the other hand, animal research suggested that nothing untoward would happen. Since the doctors had solved many of the problems leading to fetal and infant mortality, and since no maternal mortality had been reported in three years of animal testing (including primates), the DARPA project was permitted to proceed.

"We were desperate," the decision-makers said to the military historians several years later. "We believed if we hadn't done something to get more soldiers into the field, the terrorists would have overrun us. If the electromagnetic shield had not come along, there would be hundreds of thousands of clones out there." As it is, they offered, "There are only a few hundred, and we know little about how they are doing."

Although he was born a normal weight, Joe appeared to grow more quickly than the average boy. By the time he was a teenager, he had reached a height of six feet and weighed two hundred pounds. He was large but not fat. Joe's parents chose to believe that he took after his rather burly father, but when Joe reached a height of six feet, four inches, and topped 250 pounds, they grew concerned.

"No one in either of our families has ever surpassed six feet in height," his parents told the doctors. "Joe is showing no signs of stopping."

Fortunately, Joe finally topped out. Why anyone would accost him in the street or hang around when they observed his temper rising remained a mystery. Yet perhaps because Joe invited confrontation, he continued to get into scuffles. On occasion, Joe was, indeed, dangerous.

Joe wasn't a passive victim either. "No one is going to treat me like a freak because I'm blind," he seethed. On those occasions when, say, they acted nervously in his presence or spoke much too loudly, he deliberately goaded them into arguments. "What's the matter with you?" he would ask. "Can't you just treat me like a normal person?" When on the rare occasion they would confront him, Joe turned on his IVD and would jostle them just enough for him to see fear in their eyes. Then he would turn off his IVD, walk away, and smile with satisfaction. "That'll teach the assholes."

The doctors met regularly to review telemetry and in-person test results from our health checkups. "So far," Diana concluded, "all the nanobots are functioning as planned."

Dr. Arvarian added, "Everyone in the group is fine. There are no ill effects in any of them."

I felt good. I ran around town, seeing my clients with lots of energy, and even planned to retake the promotional exam. I began practicing with my IVD. "This time, I'll pass that sucker."

CHAPTER 14

Transition

As inexorably as calves break from a glacier and drop unceremoniously into the sea and float away, the "gang of four" began to drift apart. No longer bound to each other solely by blindness, our "true" differences began to emerge. With the novelty of our newfound vision waning, each member of the "gang" independently realized that he or she was no longer identifiable as either blind or sighted. We were both and neither.

In the beginning, the injustice of being categorized and thrown together so completely by a single trait had united us against the world. Now budding resentments toward each other began to pull us apart.

Not everything from the gang's newfound honesty was negative. For example, one day, Dan admitted to Joe, "I always wanted to be an athlete"—he pouted—"and here you are, born with all the right genes."

Joe uncharacteristically didn't counter punch. In an unusual act of candor, he admitted, "That's funny. I have always wanted to be more easy-going. Just like you, Dan."

"Good for you, boys," Carla interjected. "That's more forthrightness than I've seen coming from this group in a long time."

It was me who let the shoe drop first. "I think I'm going to say something none of you will like," I announced. "We have one thing in common. It's the fact that we were all so unhappy with being blind that we were willing to risk anything to be able to see. I'll bet most people in our situation are envious of people who can see. They just haven't been able to admit it the way we did, and they certainly haven't gone through what we did."

"What's so controversial about that?" Joe asked. "Of course, most of us hate being blind. The only thing is that we've been taught that it is not politically correct to admit it out loud no less do something about it."

"Well," I continued, "there's the rub. At some level, I suspect we probably all harbor at least some antipathy toward anyone who is blind, including each other."

"What are you saying?" Carla cried. "Do you mean to say we see in each other the negatives we see in ourselves? That we secretly hate each other?"

"Yes, I guess that is exactly what I'm saying," I answered, shrinking away from where Carla was sitting.

Joe piped up, "I agree. Every time we meet, I get the feeling we shouldn't be together anymore. I'm ready to get back to the world of the fully sighted. At least there, I won't have to argue with anybody about how good or how bad it is to be able to see."

Joe had said it. The gang exemplified the argument the rest of the world never thought twice about: Which was best? To see or not to see? While he wanted more eyesight than the IVD was set up to provide him, I was no longer sure I wanted any.

Joe was discontent. While he was openly a thrill seeker willing to pursue even the craziest of dreams, I had sublimated my adventurous spirit in deference to the course of least resistance. Joe didn't care what the world thought. I, on the other hand, thought it hypocritical to bow to the prejudices of what I called "visual culture." This "culture" considers it axiomatic that "the visual" is at the top of the information hierarchy, and things that are apprehended using senses other than vision are lower.

Dan held the middle ground. Grateful for the fifteen minutes of assistance the IVD afforded him, he was content with his lot. He did admit to the calming feelings he got when relieved of some of the inconveniences of not being able to see. He appreciated being able to more easily perform practical tasks like those required to do his job, go to school, or get around town. He also relished the thrill of looking at a painting and at Carla.

Carla didn't complain, but we knew she was torn between the addictive power of the sensual world revealed to her by vision and the discipline she yearned. In fact, she had figured out that turning off the IVD was a relief from the power vision held over her emotions. Perhaps something inside her knew that too much of a good thing is just as bad as not enough.

Feeling badly about the current turn of events, I attempted to backtrack. I tried to get the gang to agree to put its differences aside. "Look," I said in a conciliatory tone, "we agreed to stick together for a year, and as much as I think the doctors are being too careful, we should go along with them on this requirement. Besides, despite the differences of opinion, I've always liked you."

My declaration didn't work. Our conversation having liberated us from the subtle shackle of our group, we began to go our own way.

I was the first to miss a weekly meeting. The excuse was real; I had a promotional exam to retake.

This time, I had prepared myself. With Cheryl helping me, I found various charts and graphs in professional journal articles to look at and interpret using eyesight provided by the IVD. We even practiced how to spend only the minimum time with the IVD activated.

"Just in case they throw more at you than the last time—" Cheryl coached.

I hugged her. "You are the best," I whispered while precociously nibbling her ear.

"Concentrate," she ordered with a smile on her face.

I mused that I enjoyed looking at Cheryl more than I would have had not Carla exhorted me to enjoy it. Her smile was infectious. I smiled back.

❧

The proctor greeted me, "I remember you. Weren't you in here about a year ago?"

"Yep," I answered. "Things didn't go too well that day."

"I understand. We all have bad days. Glad you're back."

I allowed the reader, another woman on assignment from the military, to read me the instructions and questions. She acted as backup scribe to make sure I placed my answers properly in the computerized tablet. When it came time to examine charts and graphs, I waited until I could no longer decipher the information from the synthetic speech emanating from the tablet or my assistant's verbal description. In order to keep the secret of the IVD and not to surprise my attendant too much, I explained that I had a tiny pinhole of vision and pretended to sight down a narrow tunnel. I easily read the material, understood it, and nailed the answers. When the test was over, I still had five minutes of IVD left in reserve.

Gleefully, I got off the bus at my favorite bar where Cheryl awaited me. I sauntered in and, switching on the IVD just long enough to spot Cheryl with her back to me, reached my face around her and planted a kiss firmly upon her lips. The promotion was forthcoming, but the joy of getting there and sharing the victory with my sweetheart was even better.

"There are a lot of good-looking women in this place," Cheryl observed coyly.

"I'll bet there are," I remarked between sips of my favorite ale.

"Don't you want to take even a little peek?"

"Nope." I smiled. "No need. I've got what I want right here, and I'm feeling good."

❧

Joe was the next to miss a meeting. "I got caught up in a simulator exercise," he confessed. "It's beginning to look like I'll be able to do a simulated test flight pretty soon."

"Don't you think we should be talking about how the group is doing?" Carla asked indignantly. "All you can think about is flying and to hell with the rest of us. Is that it?"

"No," Joe blurted. Carla's stinging question had taken all three of us men by surprise. Recovering from the shock, Joe answered, "We risked our lives to obtain the IVDs to live better lives. I'm just doing that."

Not unexpectedly, Dan and Carla were the next ones to be truant. One day, Carla convinced Dan to take a trip to the hot springs for massages and mud baths. At another time, Dan simply wanted to stay home and sleep.

These reasons were so seemingly trivial; I began to think Dan and Carla had missed meetings to get even with Joe and me for our missing one. Worried, I called Dr. Arvarian.

"The group is nowhere as cohesive now as it was several months ago," I reported. "I think we have gotten so used to the IVD and life with it, we no longer need each other's company."

"I guess this shouldn't be a surprise," she commented. "After all, some of you barely knew each other before the Intracranial Vision Device, and you all have been living your own lives. Why shouldn't you all go your own way again? Perhaps it's a healthy sign."

"The only thing that worries me," I replied, "is that we still don't know everything there is to know about the limits of the IVD. Without each other to bounce ideas off of, I'm afraid we'll be out there with insufficient guidance."

"Try weekly phone calls instead of face-to-face meetings," the doctor suggested.

Eventually, each of us in turn found reasons to eschew even the weekly phone calls. We no longer seemed to need the counsel of the group. Unbeknown to us, we were to learn that untrodden paths not well-examined can lead to unforeseen places.

CHAPTER 15

The Beginning of the End

One day, Joe called Dr. Arvarian, "I feel like a cold is coming on. Should I do anything special?"

The doctor, suspecting nothing in particular, answered, "No, just take the usual cold medications and stay warm."

Two weeks later, Joe called her again. "This cold is not going away. I usually shake these things in three or four days. Can I come in to see the team physician?"

The blood test showed signs of something alarming. "I think we'd better bring the others in to make sure this isn't the result of the IVD procedure," Dr. Arvarian said. Turning to the physician, she added, "Please get our immunologist in here."

"This isn't the IVD procedure," the immunologist stated. "Joe is a clone. I think his immune system might be failing. Our job is to protect him from opportunistic disease until we can figure out how to stabilize his system."

Joe's sixth sense was aroused. Suspecting he might not have a lot of time left and before the team could quarantine him, he renewed his effort to find a way to fly his lighter-than-air craft. He decided that he would try no matter what, even if it meant subjecting himself to extraordinary risk.

"We're wasting time," he told Jim. "I'm ready to try this thing. How many more simulations will it take to convince everybody I can do this?"

"There's still the problem," his friend retorted, "that you haven't managed to complete the full take-off and landing sequence in under thirty minutes. You've been using up all fifteen minutes of your daily allotment of vision, and I'm afraid that the simulator is being kinder to you than Mother Nature will."

"Don't worry," Joe replied. "I've been testing the limits of the IVD, and it's giving me more than fifteen minutes. I think I can count on as many as twenty minutes a day now."

"Are you sure?" Jim asked. The instructor was convinced Joe was lying. He began to wonder if Joe had a death wish.

"Of course, I'm sure," Joe shot back. "I'm ready to give this thing a try. Let's schedule a flight."

Carla and Dan were equally adventurous but quite by accident. It is often said that there are good reasons why we possess the capacity for repression and denial. Not everything we encounter in the world is safe to keep in vivid consciousness. There are things that can shatter one's sense of security or disrupt one's sense of peace that we are better off not experiencing and certainly not reexperiencing.

Whereas Joe had experienced violence, his role in bringing it on himself had prepared him for its consequences and even steeled him against most of its psychological effect. Not so with Carla and Dan. They discovered that the ability to see some of the badness the world has to offer is not necessarily always better than being blind to it. The incident reminded Dan of a conversation he'd had with a friend a long time ago who tried to convince Dan that not everything in the world is pleasant to see and how lucky he was to be spared some of it.

One day, Carla and Dan had just left the movie theatre where, in addition to alternating their use of the IVD so they could each experience their fair share of the sexy scenes and tell the other what was happening, they had filled up on enough popcorn to squelch their dinner appetite. Carla was feeling romantic. "Let's just go home and snuggle," she cooed. "I'm not hungry."

"That's okay with me," said Dan. He thought perhaps they could go home and try to reenact some of the scenes in the movie.

Describing the sexy scenes had required them to speak in low whispers and sit very close throughout the movie. Breathing into each other's ears sent shivers down their spines. Thus, they munched popcorn to squelch their escalating libidos.

They had gone to the Saturday matinee to escape the heat of a summer day. Although dusk had fallen by the time they emerged from the theater, it was still hot. As they began the long walk back to their apartment, the thought of reentering an air-conditioned room was compelling.

"Let's cut across the park and get home as fast as we can," Dan suggested. "I know a shortcut. Don't worry," he said as an afterthought, "we won't get lost."

Carla agreed. With no sense of possible danger creeping into their minds, they turned off the sidewalk and entered the park. The area was dimly lit. Dan and Carla had not noticed; they had turned off their IVDs to preserve a few minutes in case of emergency.

It grew quiet. They held each other's arms for ease of navigation and for security. Dan used his cane and Carla her guide dog.

Suddenly, Carla's dog froze in his tracks. "What's the matter, boy?" Carla asked. She bent to pat his head. "Come on," she encouraged. "Let's go."

The dog whimpered and backed away. "What's the matter with him?" Dan asked. "He never does that."

"I don't know. There's nothing there," Carla said half to Dan and half to the dog.

"I'll go ahead and see if there's anything to be afraid of. Wait right here," Dan said. He let go of Carla's arm and proceeded forward.

Dan strained to listen for unusual sounds. Hearing nothing, he took a few more steps. Then his cane contacted a soft object.

He felt around with the tip, unable to discern what it was. "Carla," he called. "I found something lying in the path. Come here."

Dragging the whimpering dog against his will, Carla moved to where Dan stood. "Quiet," she ordered. The dog positioned himself so he wouldn't have to look at what lay on the ground beyond her.

Carla and Dan turned on their IVDS. The image coalesced slowly. They had stumbled upon a body. It lay across the path. The victim had been stabbed several times, and blood still drained from multiple wounds. The face had been pummeled, and the throat had been slit. It was a woman. Blood puddled around her.

Dan and Carla had never seen an injured body before, not even in the few movies they had gone to since receiving their IVDs. Opting for the pleasurable, their choice of movies had been kept to comedies and romances. They were unprepared for what they beheld.

"My god." They gasped in unison. "What is it?"

"It's a dead body!" Dan choked. "I think this is what happens when someone is either stabbed or shot."

Carla turned, tripped over her dog, and fell prostrate. Lifting herself to her knees and between heavy sobs, she vomited. Dan staggered backward and fought to catch his breath. His stomach did a flip-flop, and he vomited too.

Recovering his senses sufficiently to haul Carla to her feet, Dan bade Carla grab the dog, and they fled the scene. Just then, their IVDs ran out of energy, and they were plunged into a darkness deeper than they had ever experienced.

The combination of sudden vision loss with the trauma they had just experienced accentuated their distress. They kept moving until they felt they had gotten far enough away from the body to be free of the aura that seemed to surround it.

Dan and Carla couldn't put their finger on it, but something almost preternatural had them in its grip. They plowed ahead, focused so completely on fleeing the scene, they didn't realize that chaos had replaced the silence that only a moment ago had surrounded them.

Sirens blared, and people ran toward the sound of Carla's screams. Despite Dan's ministrations and exhortations to stop screaming, she had not stopped since encountering the corpse.

"Carla," Dan shouted directly into her ear. "Please be quiet. You'll cause a panic."

"I can't help it," she cried. "Something seemed terribly familiar about that person lying there."

They stopped to catch their breath. Relieved to be back in the presence of others, Carla pressed her face into Dan's shoulder and cried some more. "I guess I don't have to worry about calling the police," Dan whispered. He had begun to pull his communications tablet from his pocket when the sound of sirens broke their fugue.

That evening, Dan and Carla spent an hour with a police detective. "First," he announced, "we don't think you killed that woman. You don't seem the type, and your story about being at the movies the previous few hours checks out. Plenty of witnesses saw you enter the park only a few minutes before they saw you come running out. I guess being blind makes you stand out. Besides, you couldn't have done all that damage that quickly."

Dan and Carla hadn't processed the situation to the point where they thought they would be considered suspects, so the news didn't really relieve them. In fact, as memory of their encounter recrystallized, they grew even more upset.

"Tell me, why are you so upset? You can't see, so I assume you didn't see all the gory details."

Answering the question would have proven problematic, but the detective was already thinking about finding the true murderer and wasn't paying close attention. He sensed only that Dan and Carla could use a few minutes to collect themselves. He left the room.

"Carla," Dan whispered. "What is it you sensed about that body?"

"I think I know who she was," Carla sobbed.

"So do I," Dan choked. "I couldn't see her face because of all the blood, but I think I picked up a small wisp of perfume."

"I sensed something too," Carla replied. Hunching her shoulders and burying her face in her hands, she said in a muffled voice, "Oh god, I think it was Diana."

Dan choked back his tears. "You're right. That's who I think it was too."

"Why would anyone kill Diana?" Carla had begun sobbing again.

Dan put his arm around her shoulders and began vibrating as Carla's shivers translated through his body. "I have no idea. She was the most caring member of the development team, even more concerned for our well-being than Dr. Arvarian, if that's possible."

Carla stopped crying and raised her head with a start. "Do you think she knew something about the IVD they weren't telling us?" Then she shook even more violently than before.

Dan understood. They were both shaking now out of fear for something they couldn't quite put their finger on. "It's okay, Carla. Try to put it out of your mind."

Dan heard the detective's footsteps approaching the room. Then he remembered something else.

"Carla. Listen," he whispered quickly. "We can't tell them about the IVD," he instructed.

"What are you talking about?" she murmured; her thoughts still trapped in the fog of the ordeal.

"We can't tell the police that we actually saw the body," Dan answered. "They wouldn't believe us. Remember, to them, we are totally blind."

Carla's head straightened. "That's right," she agreed. "Not only that, we're sworn to secrecy. Besides, the cops wouldn't believe us even if we did tell them about it."

"We'll have to explain why we're so upset without telling them we saw all that blood," Dan plotted. "Obviously, they can't understand that we could be this way just because one of us felt something soft with our cane."

"The criminal justice system is notorious for its unfairness to blind people," Carla moaned. "They don't consider us as credible witnesses, even when we know exactly what happened."

"Yeah," Dan agreed. "I once heard about a blind woman who was raped. She knew exactly who the rapist was, and her testimony wasn't accepted in court. The SOB got away with it."

Carla spat, "There was more than one SOB in that courtroom."

Recovering her senses sufficiently to plot a strategy, Carla suggested they simply tell the police that they tripped over the body, and it freaked them out.

"That's it!" Dan whispered exuberantly. "We'll tell them that in tripping over the body, we didn't touch it with our hands. That will explain why we're not covered in blood. We can say that it seemed gross just the same. That's pretty much the truth anyway."

"Should we tell them who we think it is?"

"No," Dan answered emphatically. "If we say anything, they'll want to know how we know Diana."

Carla agreed, "Okay, we'll stick to the story about why we're upset and say nothing else. That should satisfy them."

The police were much gentler with them than Dan and Carla expected. After hearing their story, the officer thanked them for finding the body and offered them a ride home.

In the police car, Carla clung tightly to Dan's arm and didn't release it until she felt the car turn into the security area in front of their complex. They were home.

A police woman drove. "You've had quite an evening," she declared. When Dan and Carla remained silent, she added, "Don't worry, the questioning is over. We know you had nothing to do with the murder. In fact, we've already made a solid arrest."

"Really?" Dan gasped. "How could you do that so fast?"

"Oh, we picked up a fellow of questionable national origin jogging away from the scene. We've got him for interrogation. It's possible he didn't know the victim but was hired to perform the kill."

Carla and Dan groaned and then remained silent. The car stopped. They relaxed. "How do you get used to seeing these things every day?" Dan asked.

"Most of us never see something that awful," the officer answered. "For those who do and are bothered by it, we have counseling."

"I'd imagine anyone seeing a dead body would need counseling," Carla murmured.

"We are prepared for these things by our training," the detective answered. "Still, there's nothing like the real thing. All the film and discussion in the world don't prepare you, as well as that first experience."

The detective turned off the engine. "Here we are, safe and sound." She got out, opened the door for her guests, and stepped back.

Dan and Carla scrambled from the car. Saying goodbye, they hurried inside and locked the door.

Carla fell into Dan's arms and began to cry again. "How will we ever get this out of our minds?" she asked. "We didn't have any training, and we don't have a trauma therapist. And why did it have to be Diana?"

In a fruitless effort to cleanse themselves of the sordid event, Dan and Carla decided to take long showers. "Maybe we can wash this off of us and out of our minds," Carla explained as she gave Dan a gentle push away, signaling her need for some alone time.

"I think you're right," Dan replied. "Let's get cleaned up."

They emerged from their showers physically clean but still shaken. In a more desperate effort to rid themselves of the stain etched into their minds, they consumed a bottle of wine. Then they hit upon an idea. They would distract themselves by making love, thinking they could replace trauma with pleasure. Things didn't work out the way they hoped.

As for me, I had a mind-wrenching experience of a different kind. Mine took place deep in the recesses of the unconscious. During one of our heated conversations, Joe had accused me of succumbing to the difficulties of blindness and letting my dreams wither away. His words bothered me. I began to do a lot of soul-searching. "Was Joe right?" I asked myself. Had I put my most fundamental desires so far into the scrap heap of lost hopes that I'd forgotten they were there?

A stirring began to surface. At first, only a rumbling in the pit of my stomach, the feeling seemed like a yearning for something deep, suppressed a long time ago and almost lost from memory. Soon realizing just how unsatisfied with my life I'd been, the stirring fluoresced into anger. My attempt to seek out the roots of this ill-defined dissatisfaction would lead to a strange place.

It started with a question I'd often been asked. "When you dream, are you able to see?"

People ask this question with a degree of earnestness that suggests that it is common sense that everyone must see in their dreams. It's as if there is a tacit assumption about these things. It reminded me of my youth when I felt left out of social circles, and everyone else knew things I didn't seem to know.

I would always answer the same way. "No. When I dream, it's just like when I'm awake. In truth, half the time. I don't even remember my dreams."

My answer always seemed to leave them unsatisfied. They appeared disappointed to hear that my dreams were mainly auditory—a little touch, and occasionally some taste or smell, I'm not sure, and no sight. It was as if they hoped there is redemption in the world of the unconscious, and that redemption for the blind took the form of eyesight.

It was as if they imagined in the unconscious any fantasy can come true, including the creation of light from darkness. It seemed unfathomable to them that I would insist that without the raw materials of visual imagery, it is as impossible to form a visible picture in your head as it is to change lead into gold.

Their doubts made me think. *Perhaps I am once again taking the easy way out. Maybe there is more.*

Slowly it coalesced that I was haunted by the notion that once upon a time, I might have possessed vision. I had always assumed that I had none. Hadn't the screening tests Dr. Arvarian conducted prior to the IVD surgery proven this assumption correct? Still I mulled, *I wonder. Was I able to see as a fetus?*

"The light at the end of the tunnel in near-death experiences might be a memory we have from the time of our birth." I wrote in my diary. "Perhaps seeing the path to the outside of the womb is our first visual experience. In the end, it might be the most glorious image we will ever see." Then I smiled and wrote. "And at the end of life, it might also be the last image we ever see."

I continued writing: "Might it be possible that we are programmed with archetypal images passed down through the ages from our ancestors? Let's agree that our minds represent the experiential portion of our existence, our souls. Although the debate that our minds emerge tabula rasa from the womb rages on. That is, without knowledge, there certainly is no doubt that our physical brains are preprogrammed to some extent."

My thoughts continued. "If by 'seeing,' we mean the ability of our brains and minds to make sense of input from our eyes, what makes it possible for us to be born with that ability? Must not we be born with our brains ready to recognize at least basic input? Otherwise, how could we begin to make sense even of the most primitive things we see when we first open our eyes as newborns?"

I wrote: "Surely the brain must have the ability to see before we are born. Suppose visual images existed in my brain from the time of, say, my third trimester in the womb? Is it possible that my dreams could reflect these images? Would I be 'seeing' in my dreams? Was I abnormal if I didn't? Perhaps there is some truth in the conventional wisdom that all of us have the potential to relate to visual images."

I began to imagine I once had vision dreams. Long neglect had caused them to fade into oblivion, tucked away so deeply that even Dr. Arvarian's screening tools could not pick them up.

More vexing after years of sightlessness—or was it my willingness simply to accept my lot—I had lost my appreciation for the fact that there is more to life than what is within my immediate grasp. I thought, *Is Joe's unorthodoxy his way of counteracting the stultification to which I have allowed myself to succumb?*

I panicked. "I'd become boring. Where had my dreams gone? Were they hiding in the recesses of my mind? Or have I lost them forever?"

In a desperate attempt to learn the answer and, in the same effort, to recover a sense of hope for the future, I called a psychiatrist to whom I could reveal my soul. In that moment, I decided to reveal the IVD to the psychiatrist, an "outsider."

In the months when the "gang of four" still met with the team, Diana had unsuspectingly turned my head around. On one level, she probably knew exactly what she was doing. I had a crush on her, and she must have known it. Although she maintained outwardly a clinical distance, I believe she was flattered by the extra attention I paid her during our meetings.

"Diana," I'd say. "Tell us about your research."

"It's top secret, and you know it," she would rejoin. "Why do you keep asking me?"

"Because I love hearing your voice," I'd quip. The banter would continue for a few minutes, and usually Carla would break in with a chastising comment about my disloyalty to Cheryl, and I would slump into silence.

In our discussions, I couldn't help thinking that Diana seemed to want to talk more but held back.

One day, I decided to confront her. I used my IVD to follow her to her car. Without asking permission, I simply sat on her front bumper and waited.

"What are you doing?" she asked a bit too impatiently.

"Why, Diana," I answered. "Is that any way to treat one of your offspring?"

Alarmed at the reference to the term she always used when talking about her nanobots, she grew cautious. "What do you mean? You're not my offspring."

"Well," I said as I moved to the driver's side window. "Isn't the gang of four part of a clinical trial? Doesn't that make us as much a product of your work as the little bugs in our heads?"

"Be serious," she snapped. The engine of her new hydrogen-powered car whirred to life.

"I am being serious," I remonstrated. "Please talk to me."

I moved in front of the car to block her way. "I won't let you go until you tell me what it is you're not telling us."

She threw the car into reverse and backed away from me. Turning to leave, she called in a loud whisper, "My offspring have a lot more going for them that you can imagine."

She drove off, leaving me stunned. What did she mean? What would I tell the others? Should I reveal the conversation to Dr. Arvarian? What might happen to Diana if she had just breeched protocol, and someone found out about it?

I asked the psychiatrist, "Can you help me find myself?"

He bade me to tell him what was on my mind.

I told him about the hollow place in my heart, and that I couldn't shake the feeling that there was much more to what made me tick than I could grasp hold of. I told him about my sordid life as a blind person and my trek to short-term vision via the IVD. I said

I hoped that my recent experience with eyesight had awakened my mind to the possibilities. I related how, as a result, I had been vainly seeking on my own to dredge up any visual images my primal mind might be hiding.

"I have some thoughts on how to help you," he said after listening to my story. "I suggest regressive hypnosis. I will plant the suggestion that you should see these images if they are there in your nightly dreams."

The psychiatrist proposed that I might be suffering from a sense of abandonment. If I could see my mother's face, he suggested, I would no longer feel this way. He hypothesized that my adult psyche was permeated with a deep sense of disconnectedness from the world around me.

"Perhaps," he suggested, "reestablishing a connection to your mother will make things better."

"My mother didn't abandon me," I protested. "She took care of me. In fact, she would be taking care of me still if I were to live at home."

"I have no doubt your mother has always loved and cherished you. It is possible," he explained, "that when your mother discovered you couldn't see, she was frightened for a while. At a crucial portion of the development of your personality, she may have unknowingly withdrawn some affection, moving away from you emotionally. This would explain the longing that you feel as an adult."

Growing angry at the thought that my mother would have considered me a monster, I blurted, "Why would she do that?"

The doctor continued. "I'm sure your mother loved you," he said with assurance. "Like most people, she no doubt had little or no experience with, shall we say, a son with your unique qualities. She simply didn't know what to do. For example, most parents are taught that they should interact with their infants by holding them and looking into their eyes for feedback. You couldn't help it, but you did not provide her with the kind of connection she needed at that moment."

Sensing my distress, he tried to comfort. "Your inability to respond to her face with expression may have made your mother back away from you just enough to give you the unconscious sense of emptiness you feel today."

Seeing that I was about the burst into tears, he quickly continued, "Don't worry. From the way you appear to feel about your mother and your capacity for contemplativeness and emotion, I can assume she recovered quickly. It seems to me that your mother eventually learned to connect with you in many ways."

"But, doc," I exclaimed. "We don't all walk around feeling this way." My observation seemed to come from a bitter place. "Carla feels loved, and Dan seems content."

"That's right," the doctor admitted. "Everyone's experiences are different. Perhaps their parents were not as initially frightened by what they saw in Carla and Dan. Perhaps Dan and Carla were born with a more expressive temperament than you. Perhaps their parents were more outgoing than yours to begin with. There is a great deal of evidence to show that we inherit, if not our personalities, then at least our temperaments. The combination of more outgoing parents connecting with more extraverted children might have prevented the potential loss caused by lack of sight."

"And what about me?"

"You are less outgoing by nature," he said gently. "That only means that your mother, who may have needed a little more comforting herself, didn't quite react to you the way Dan's and Carla's mothers reacted to them. The shame of it is that it doesn't have to be this way," the doctor continued. "Parent training can help new mothers give their blind children the degree of contact they need, if only there were enough teachers out there."

The doctor's voice trailed off. I grew angry again. This time, my anger stemmed from the injustice of neglect that exists in a world where so many resources are expended on destruction and so few on helping people. Shaking off my gloom, I asked, "Well, doctor, what can we do to help me now?"

"Let's try hypnosis," the doctor said. "I'll make several suggestions that I hope will trigger old memories. Your job is to force yourself to wake up after every dream to write down what you remember."

More motivated than ever to be free of my "damaged personality," I immersed myself in the project. Although I followed his instructions to the letter, nothing visual materialized, that is, until the end.

In the meantime, he made a call to Dr. Arvarian.

"Thanks for letting me know," she said. "Just go easy with the hypnosis," she cautioned. "We don't know how he'll react."

"I'll keep you posted," the psychiatrist assured. "By the way," he added almost aimlessly. "He seems to be quite fond of your assistant. I believe he said her name is Diana."

"I'll let her know," Dr. Arvarian said. Her tone was measured and flat.

Machiavelli rationalized. We, on the other hand, should question. Should we accept the inevitabilities of pursuing our vision dreams?

CHAPTER 16

The End

Joe was the first casualty. At one of our telephone meetings, he informed us that he was about to try flying his lighter-than-air craft and thought he could stretch his IVD well past the daily fifteen-minute limit. He'd been trying to do this for a while and thought he'd managed to maintain vision for as much as twenty minutes.

"How do you know for sure that you really can see for more than fifteen minutes?" I persisted. "For all you know, you could be seeing afterimages or just engaging in wishful thinking."

"Get off my back!" he shot back. "I know what I'm seeing is real. The IVD is more powerful than they told us. Don't you think that's possible? I know I can do this."

Then he added, "I don't see why we have the fifteen-minute limit anyway. Why can't we keep using the IVD all the time?"

"The doctor explained it to us," I said, growing exasperated. "Don't you remember? Or don't you want to believe? The robotic implants are constantly discharging energy and moving from place to place in our brains. They need to recharge their energy cells after a short amount of use."

"Do you have to do this solo?" Dan asked. "Why can't the glider be controlled from the ground?"

"It's a glider, Dan," Joe answered with exasperation. "The whole idea is to be one with the wind. It's the most natural form of flying there is. It's as close to being like a bird as you can get."

"You're really going to risk your life for this?" Carla's voice easily betrayed her anxiety.

"Yes," Joe answered. "Please don't worry, Carla. It's only a matter of time before I try. And I have to try."

The time finally arrived.

"Okay, Joe," Jim called over the radio. "The weather reports say it's a go. Prepare for takeoff."

"Ready." Joe adjusted his headset. "I hear you loud and clear," he called into his radio.

The towplane accelerated down a short runway, yanking Joe and his balsa-light aircraft behind it. The ground bumped under him for a few seconds, and then just as the simulator had constructed, the plane lifted from the ground. Everything went smooth and silent. Joe was airborne.

"Turning to port," the towplane pilot announced. Joe felt his left wing dip, and as gravity forced him to lean with his craft, he countered by tensing the muscles on the right side of his body. Gusts of air buffeted his craft as it ascended over the cliffs that lined the ocean shore below him.

"I'm turning to the right," came the next announcement. Joe's body followed his plane into the lean. He was getting used to the sound of the air outside his flimsy cockpit. He felt the adrenalin rush that comes with risk. It did not dawn on him that perhaps he was enjoying the rush a bit too much even for his lust for danger. Instead he thought, *There's no turning back now*. All he could think about was staying over the drafts. He was fixated on only one thing: Fulfilling his dream of soaring like a bird.

"Releasing in five seconds," the tow pilot announced.

Joe felt an unexpected fear in the pit of his belly.

"This is it," he said to himself. "I'm on my own."

The towrope disconnected, and Joe's plane immediately dropped toward the ground. "Turn on your radar!" The cry came from Joe's instructor on the ground. "What's going on in your head? For God's sake, remember your training."

Joe switched on his radar and tuned into the ground beacons that would guide him to a smooth landing site. "Radar reading updrafts," he shouted. "Sorry about that, Jim," he said sheepishly into his microphone. "I guess I've been preoccupied lately."

"Get with the program, Joe," his instructor called. "A lapse like that will get you killed."

"Okay," Joe replied. "I'm turning to the left. I think there's an updraft over there."

The updraft Joe thought he'd find to his port was, indeed, there, but it seemed to catch only his left wing.

"You didn't turn enough," Jim called. "The draft looks to be at your eleven o'clock."

Joe turned more to port. The plane shuddered and began to drop again. The radar was not picking up the birds well enough.

"Is your IVD turned on?" Jim shouted. "Follow the birds. You're still only skirting the updraft. You're losing altitude. The updrafts seem to be swirling. They are changing fast. Follow the birds."

Joe switched on the IVD. He had not turned it on, hoping to extend his vision as long as possible. Fighting off his initial panic, Joe tried to execute Jim's command. Spotting a flock of birds to his left and below him, he turned the plane in that direction. The draft caught his wings and pushed the plane high into the air. Joe and the entire ground crew breathed a sigh of relief. Perhaps this was going to work after all.

Joe soared above the cliffs. He looked down and around, soaking in the view he had been waiting to see all his life. The ocean water sparkled far ahead. Then the cliffs moved under him. Joe watched, fascinated as he and the birds swooped first left and then right. The cliff held their place, challenging Joe to hover above their sharp rocks and crags for as long as he dared.

Joe decided to follow the birds that flew closest to the cliff's edges. He pointed his nose downward, and his craft glided toward the precipices. In an exact imitation of his avian idles and disregarding calls from his ground crew to increase his altitude, Joe swooped toward the ocean. The rocky terrain that had preoccupied Joe's gaze for the previous few minutes was replaced by white sandy beaches. Then gliding out over open water, Joe saw nothing but the deep blue sea beneath him.

Drifting into rapture, Joe thought, *I could fly this way forever. Everything I've ever wanted, I have now.*

Joe may have known he was slipping into an altered state of mind, but he didn't care. He also may have realized that his time was growing short, but the knowledge didn't seem to bother him. The radio cracked. "Joe, for heaven's sake, turn the plane around. You're too far out."

Joe tried to shake himself free of the reverie, but something seemed to hold him back. "I could just fly forever," he said into the radio. "No more worries, nothing to worry about."

"Joe!" The command from ground control was loud and stern. "Get back here and get down. Now!"

Jim had seen the phenomenon once before. "Pilot suicide," he gasped. "He's going to let himself crash."

To Jim's relief, his friend turned the plane in a hard circle to the right. Again, to the relief of everyone on the ground, an updraft caught Joe's wings. Then instead of a smooth ascent and without warning, the plane shot high into the sky.

G-forces pressed Joe hard against the back of his seat. His plane climbed in a high arching trajectory. Joe's IVD showed him deep blue sky with a few puffy clouds. "So that's what angels look like," he mumbled.

Hearing his words and growing alarmed, the ground crew radioed to Jim from their various positions beneath Joe's flight path, "Jim, for God's sake, get him down!"

Jim was already on it. "Joe," he yelled. "Are you okay? Talk to me. Joe, level off!"

The draft subsided, and Joe's course turned into a parabola. The plane crested, and the nose pitched over. Like a hawk spotting carrion, Joe and his dream ship dove at a steep angle.

"I can't control this," Joe moaned into the microphone. "I think I'm finished." He looked out his cockpit window to see the last precipice disappear below him. Only white sand dappled with occasional boulders stretched before him.

"Joe," cried his instructor. "Why are you giving up? Try anything. Turn to the right. I see some birds over to your right. Turn to the right!"

The plane pitched hard. The right wing dropped beyond a safe angle, terminating its dip only when it pointed straight toward the ground.

An unpowered plane cannot fly this way. Its wings must present as large a profile to the updrafts as possible. Moreover, the pressure on Joe's body grew unbearable. It took all of his strength just to hold his head upright. He felt the plane rapidly descend. Everyone in the ground crew, including Jim, began to panic.

"Joe!" Jim screamed. "Roll! Roll!"

Assuming he heard his instructions, Jim hoped Joe could return the plane's wings to a horizontal position. He hoped that even if Joe ended up upside down, the plane would pick up enough air to stop its plummet. It was a long shot. Worse, the instructor knew desperate thoughts like these signified that his student was in a grave situation.

A long second passed. Nothing happened. Then to his horror, his friend saw Joe's plane disappear over the cliff line. The ground crew screamed in unison. Their echoes died, and for a moment, there was silence. The next sound, a muffled thud, signified the impact.

If Joe had any last words, none of them heard. Only the birds, Joe's kindred spirits, witnessed his final moment. Later, telemetry showed that Joe had not keyed his radio, making no final attempt to reach out to his friends. However, he did not die alone. The winged creatures who accompanied him to his end bore witness. Along with the birds, the nanobots inside Joe's head also recorded the event.

Nanobot telemetry proved Joe right about something else. The IVD did not terminate after fifteen minutes. Fully twenty-five minutes into his flight, they gave Joe what must have been his final image. While in a rapid plummet, I somehow know he saw blue sky, white sand, several birds, the shadow of his craft, and then nothing.

Carla and Dan, star-crossed lovers, met their end next, and in a way I thought most unfair. According to the biopsychological autopsy, Carla and Dan thought it would be great to make love the way they'd seen people do in the movies. The day had been a rough one, stumbling upon Diana's body and ending up in a police station—and all this after a lusty time at the movies.

They consumed a bottle of wine and eased onto the couch. Dan reached for Carla to take her into his arms. When Carla reciprocated, Dan whispered in his most husky voice, "Let's look deep into each other's eyes."

What transpired next makes me wonder whether people were truly meant to see as much as I had thought. With their hands, Dan and Carla traced the lines of each other's faces. "Let's gaze into each other's eyes," Dan suggested again. He felt her nod, signaling approval.

Knowing they hadn't given the IVDs enough time to fully regenerate since turning them off a few hours ago, they nonetheless activated them. Their power began flowing almost immediately. While their brains eagerly received the calming effect of the wine, the IVDs, seemingly overenergized, began to lose their inhibitions. Suddenly and for reasons still unknown, there was an energy spike.

The robotic implants inside Carla and Dan's heads tried to oblige their owners' wish to gaze deeply into each other's eyes. Feeling the heat of the moment, the nanobots' activity level escalated out of control.

Not only that, in accordance with their programming, the process of transferring the trauma in the park to long-term memory had already begun. Mobile nanobots, doing the work of memory consolidation began meeting resistance from forces trying to prevent implantation of the images. Thus, "innocent" nanobots, going about their regular business, became combatants in an unplanned cerebral civil war.

Dan and Carla's intense feelings may have caused the robots to overload. As they grew more animated on the couch, they did not notice that something was going terribly wrong with their IVDs. Nanobots began frantically moving toward each other, lusting after what could only be interpreted as a microscopic version of what their masters were doing outside.

Rushing toward each other like lemmings toward a precipice, the now hyperactive electrodes began to collide in orgasmic delirium, more or less in imitation of their corporeal hosts. Tragically for their masters, the wayward nanobots disintegrated, spraying their silicon debris hither and yon. The massive disruption within their craniums caused Carla and Dan to suffer fatal strokes.

I comfort myself in the thought that Carla and Dan must have been immensely happy in their final moment. The report said they died with peaceful expressions upon their faces.

One thing puzzles me though. According to the memory files extracted from the robotic implants at autopsy, while they made love, except for an initial penetrating gaze into each other's eyes, Carla and Dan didn't look at each other's bodies—not even once. They could have, their IVDs, although they should not have had enough power, still reported sufficient energy to have enabled them to do so.

Perhaps their sense of touch was enough for them, and they didn't want to risk spoiling it by distracting themselves with unnecessary input. Clearly, they were so involved in what they were doing it didn't matter.

Had the IVDs begun to grow more powerful than intended? Had the doctors, as Joe suspected, not told us the whole truth about the technology they had transferred into our bodies? Was our endeavor really part of the war effort? Had Dr. Arvarian sold out to the military after all? Most painful, had the prospect of vision blinded us to a truth that we should have seen?

We had certainly agreed to embrace the power of even a little bit of eyesight. That is why, I'm sure, I ignored my instincts about whether this was morally or ethically right. One way or the other, we willingly bought into the scheme. I thought, *We are well down the rabbit hole now.*

Meanwhile and with no portent of bad tidings, I had been building toward my own denouement. In the ensuing months after my visit to the psychiatrist, I'd continued to make my weekly pilgrimages to his office for debriefing and renewal of the hypnogogic suggestions the doctor had planted in my head. I told him about my dreams, lamenting that as yet none of them had been visual.

"I'm surprised," he said. "You are using the IVD, aren't you?"

"Yes," I answered. "But I'm averaging only about ten minutes per day. Each time I figure out what something looks like or where something is located, I instantly memorize it and don't need to use the IVD anymore."

"Has your lifestyle remained constant?" the doctor asked.

"Yes," I answered. "Why do you ask?"

"You haven't felt the need to use the IVD to handle strange and new challenges?"

"Not too often lately."

"That might explain why your current visual experiences have not begun transferring into your dreams."

The doctor explained that my hesitation to be adventurous, even with the IVD providing eyesight to make things easier, might be only the latest manifestation of why I had come to see him.

"You asked me to help you become more free, to help you widen your horizons." He seemed to be scolding me. "Your hesitance to use the IVD is thwarting the very process that might do just that. Try stretching yourself."

"Why haven't I seen anything in my dreams?" I pursued.

"You are not storing enough visual experience to nourish your dream world." Then he asked, "Isn't there anything you dreamed about doing as a child? Some fantasy you spent time imagining? Something that saddens you to think about because it hurts so much?"

"That's an interesting question," I replied. "I haven't thought about it for a long time, but I used to imagine being able to play major league baseball. How's that for an impossible dream?"

"Not bad," the doctor answered with alacrity. "I think it's time for you to revisit that fantasy. What could you do to reinvigorate the dream?"

"That's easy, doc," I replied. "I could get my girlfriend to go with me to a ball game. We'd get ground-level seats near home plate. I'd use my IVD to see the game and pretend I'm actually on the playing field. That'll get my imagination going."

The doctor endorsed my idea and sent me on my way. I felt excited. A few weeks later, the ball game etched in my head; I had a dream.

A right-hand batter faced a lefty on the mound. He looked around, taking in with a single sweep the stands rising above him on all sides, the first-base dugout, and the wall and warning track that circumscribed the field. The grass was deep green and the dirt a delectable orange. The bases and chalk lines were pearly white. This was a high-impact item as all he'd ever experienced was the washed out and unattended crosswalk markings on the streets of an unkempt city.

Now I was the batter. The pitcher seemed far away and small. Standing in the batter's box, somehow the view didn't look right. *There's no way I'll ever see the ball*, I thought.

Gritting my teeth, I cursed under my breath. "What am I doing here? It serves me right for trying something like this." I steeled myself to hang in there.

Until that moment, my only previous experiences seeing a pitcher on the mound were the view from the stands with Cheryl and the few games I had watched on television since getting my IVD. These bore no resemblance to what I should now be seeing from the batter's box. Unfortunately, there was no time to decipher the discrepancy. The pitcher was about to throw.

The ball flew toward me. At the last moment, it appeared as a blip emerging from the whirling dervish that was the pitcher. Before I could move a muscle, the ball smacked bullet-fast and rock-hard into the catcher's mitt. The umpire called the strike.

As he prepared for his next delivery, the pitcher looked even smaller and farther away. My bat felt leaden in my hands. I shivered, convinced that I wouldn't be able to swing, no less make contact. Then I heard my mother call to me. "You can do it, son."

Was my dream telling me it was time to connect with her?

The next pitch sped my way. I saw it coming. That was a good sign. Notwithstanding, it whizzed past me with another thud.

"Ball," cried the umpire.

I allowed myself a distraction. I'd heard Ted Williams could see the stitches of the ball as it rotated toward him. *Pay attention*, I thought. *You'll be lucky to survive this without a concussion.*

With a better sense of when the next pitch would come, I dared turn my head and look toward my mother's voice. "Mom," I called. "Is that really you?"

"Yes, son," she answered. "I'm here, but you don't really need me."

"I need you more than I've ever needed you," I called. "Where have you been, Mom?"

"I've always been here. Open your heart, and you will always feel me near you. You don't need me, son. Go ahead and hit that ball."

The pitcher wound up, the image did not blur this time, and the ball streaked in my direction.

Somehow, I guessed correctly that the pitch would be right down the middle. I swung level and, with all my might. I crushed it.

On contact, the ball felt amazingly soft. I'd expected it to feel hard, the way my cane did when striking cement or metal, stinging with the vibration of one hard object colliding with another. There was no sting. I'd apparently hit the ball on the "sweet spot" of the bat.

The crowd roared. I remembered I was supposed to run. As I circled the bases, I thought, *So this is what it's like!*

Rounding third and looking ahead, I peered into the stands. I saw my mother's face, beatific and shining brighter than the rest. I ran toward it. Tears blurred my vision. I was bathed in warmth. I heard her voice again. "I knew you could do it."

I prepared to rush toward the light of her face. Remembering my duty, I stomped my foot hard upon home plate. Triumphant, I looked up, but her face was gone. Instead, I was enveloped in blinding white light. Then the world exploded.

EPILOGUE

Still in the Universe

"Flatline! We've got a flatline!"

"Doctor, may I assist?"

Somehow, there she was. Dr. Arvarian had scrubbed in and stood ready to take over.

"Damn it! It's over," the sweat-soaked doctor said.

The neuro-ophthalmologist shoved him aside. "Not yet, it isn't," she cursed. Muttering to herself, she said, "We didn't retain the experiences of all four of them in this one only to have his brain fried by some ridiculous hypnogogic malarkey."

Dr. Arvarian held a device over my head. It contained no probes, no lasers, in fact, nothing that appeared relevant to the emergency at hand. She activated the device, and an electromagnetic force field formed around my head. The energy field, only an angstrom or two above my scalp, instantly singed my hair. The field frequencies, although invisible, seemed to get the attention of the nanobots.

As she held the device, Dr. Arvarian exhorted, "Come on. Deactivate."

The nanobots seemed to hear her. Those that were heading there ceased their charge toward my brain stem. Troops in the rear guard halted their helter-skelter melee throughout the rest of my cerebrum.

Microscopic laser shut down. Cilia stiffened. Neurotransmitters stopped squirting. The microelectrodes had come to rest.

Soldiers charged in. They hustled the hospital staff from the emergency room and whisked Dr. Arvarian and me away.

"Where to, doc?" the lieutenant asked.

"To the DARPA cryo center," she ordered. Clearly, the neuro-ophthalmologist had a plan.

I had a dream which was not all a dream. Byron.

Am I dreaming now? Am I dead? In suspended animation? Were those months when I used the IVD an illusion? The image of my mother in my dream, whether it was real or not, has cast doubt in my mind over how all of us relate to the universe. Is it possible, for example, that something as primal as the connection to one's mother cannot be accounted for solely by one's senses? If there had never been an image of my mother deep in my neurons for the nanobots to find, how did I manage to construct such an idealized image of her? What I know for sure is that no matter how your mother reaches you, there is no substitute for her love.

Funny thing, when I heard her voice and saw her face, I thought my mother would say she wanted me to come home. Instead, she told me the opposite. Far from feeling rejected and bathed in the feeling of her warmth for the first time in my life, I felt safe.

The dream of having vision now seems like a dream itself, and I can't be certain that it actually happened. I now reside somewhere in the universe, and even though I don't know where, I am not lost. Everything seems as it should be. Finally at peace, I dare to sleep. If by chance I dream, I'll dream about freedom.

And may you also find freedom. May the land in which you live nourish and protect you and not at the expense of others. May the world remain open and not sequestered within boundaries of fear. For when people are afraid, there is no telling what they will do.

REFERENCES

G.G. Byron (Lord). (2019). "Darkness". Poetry Foundation. https://www.poetryfoundation.org/poems/43825/darkness-56d222aeeee1b.

J. Dryden (2019). "Dreams are but interludes, which fancy makes;..." in Goodreads Romance Week. https://www.goodreads.com/quotes/1325545-dreams-are-but-interludes-which-fancy-makes-when-monarch-reason.

H.D. Thoreau (2019). "Our truest life is when we are in our dreams awake." Henry David Thoreau Quotes—BrainyQuote. https://www.brainyquote.com/authors/henry_david_thoreau.

G. Santayana (2019). Internet Encyclopedia of Philosophy. https://www.iep.utm.edu/santayan/#content.

ABOUT THE AUTHOR

Vision Dreams: A Parable

Born with a severe visual impairment, Anthony Candela went to school and had a successful professional career, competed in sports and dabbled in many hobbies—all this while slowly going blind. It was while convalescing from a broken arm at age 12 he read his first astronomy book. About that time his fascination with science fiction was cemented with the advent of two TV shows: "Lost in Space" and "Star Trek". Studies in science and mathematics rounded out the background that undergirds this novella. Losing his eyesight and the post-911 era drove him to the keyboard.

Mr. Candela is a "retired" athlete (wrestler and long distance runner). He loves movies, sports, reading, writing, and music, dabbling in guitar. As a practical matter, he would gladly take on fifteen minutes of vision per day as a supplement to his skills as a blind person. Likewise, he would gladly use the few minutes of fame this book might provide to promote an open, honest and just society.

CPSIA information can be obtained
at www.ICGtesting.com
Printed in the USA
FSHW011618011219

9 781098 006730